confessions:

FACT or FICTION ?

Chrysalis Editorial (www.chrysaliseditorial.com)
Washington, D.C.
2010

"The End of the Season" first appeared in the story collection *Slipping the Moorings* published in 2009 by Entasis Press.

Cover design by Amanda Vacharat

Cover photograph courtesy of the estate of Aristedes Nicolau

First Edition

confessions:

FACT or FICTION ?

φ

a collection of short stories and memoir

Edited by Herta B. Feely & Marian O'Shea Wernicke
Chrysalis Editorial, Washington, D.C.
www.chrysaliseditorial.com

Chrysalis Editorial, Washington, D.C.
www.chrysaliseditorial.com

contents

introduction

WELL KNOWN IS THE FACT that authors use fictional elements in their memoirs and, conversely, dip their quills into the real stuff of their lives when penning short stories and novels. Regardless, it would seem that there is a clear division between the two genres. But is there and can you tell the difference?

When the hullabaloo emerged over James Frey's literary fraud— he'd liberally sprinkled his memoir (*A Million Little Pieces*) with fiction —I was struck by the fact that originally he had attempted to sell the book as a novel, failed, then succeeded in pawning it off as memoir. Not only did *A Million Little Pieces* do well, but it rose into the rarefied realm of Oprah bookdom, hit the New York Times bestseller list, and sold millions of copies! What did this mean? That a story like Frey's is juicier and hence more marketable as non-fiction?—judging by the agents and publishers' interest in the "memoir" version, I think that's a yes. Does that mean we are inherently more fascinated by a "true" story than a fictional one? That probably depends on the nature of the story, but that's also a yes if it's gritty, sexy, revealing.

In any case, I began to think about how readers can tell the difference between a "made up" story and a "true" story—can we sniff out a fictional paragraph in an otherwise real event? Are there any telltale signs?

I spoke with writers about the increasingly blurred lines between "fact and "fiction" and the liberties we take in mixing memoir and fiction. (Some of their responses are included below.) The more I learned, the more I wanted to explore the boundary between the two forms and the reader's experience of it. So I set about compiling an anthology comprised of short stories and memoir without revealing the stories' genres where they appear in the book, instead providing the answers in a key at the back.

My hope is to engage you, the reader, in this subject. I invite you to examine whether you wanted a story to be true or false. Did you feel betrayed when you were wrong? Did you ever feel tricked? When reading these pieces, notice the words, phrases, and paragraphs; the actions, dialogue, and scenes that prompt you to question whether the piece is fiction or fact. What are the clues? Is it something about the author's style, the point-of-view, an event that just has to be true, or one that couldn't possibly be?

Along with the key, our authors discuss the genesis of their stories and their thoughts on the issue of fact vs. fiction, allowing you to gain insight into the author's writing and your responses to the stories, and also to examine the accuracy and validity of your instincts and guesses.

Our assistant Amanda Vacharat tells this fascinating <u>true</u> anecdote:

I'm at a writing conference. On the stage, a quivering 15-year-old boy is accepting his award for Best High School Short Fiction.

"Well, the boy (David) says, "I was inspired by my summer job. The park where the boy in my story works – that's where I worked. All the characters in the story, too – they're based on people I met there."

The audience is nodding – I'm nodding, the runner-ups on the stage behind him are nodding, the judges are nodding. We recognize David's impulse to draw fiction from real life, to use "facts" as a springboard. Now we are waiting to hear how he used this inspiration to generate his winning story.

He leans in closer to the microphone, as if about to give it a kiss. "In fact," he says, voice shaking, "everything in the story is real. It's all true. All of it actually happened. None of it is made up."

Silence. Everyone has stopped nodding. I can feel the unified question rising into an angry bubble toward this poor kid: If his story is TRUE, shouldn't he be disqualified? Is it fair for him to win?

The woman next to me looks confused. Shoulders tighten. A runner-up squirms like she's about to cry. David shrinks into his too-big suit, quickly thanks the audience, and runs off the stage, suddenly aware of the crime he's committed.

Welcome to the world of fiction, David. To be fair, David's story was a first person narrative about a boy's thoughts as he parks people's cars and imagines them into old age. Surely those thoughts qualify as fiction? Okay, so was his story fiction based on "an experience he had" or does it belong in the domain of memoir? I'll let you decide.

Following are a few varied, often conflicting thoughts on the subject of fact vs. fiction from authors whose stories you are about to read:

"Sometimes they'll ask what it's like to write fiction and nonfiction. As if there's some great divide between the two. The dirty little secret? They are much closer aligned than we often care to acknowledge." –Tim Wendel

"The Sonoran desert is part of the United States. It is also part of Mexico. But whichever side of the border you're on, it's still the desert. That's what I think about fact or fiction. Makes no difference. It's the story that counts, and the line has been blurry from day one." –George Nicholas

"Fiction, so often, is heavily infused with fact, though I'd argue the best stories free themselves of the 'facts' at some point and, instead, adhere to the rules of the world of the story." –R. Dean Johnson

"I write only fiction these days, in part because I've grown less and less interested in trying to separate actual experience from imagined experience. As a fiction writer, I don't need to remain "true" to anything but the story, and I can use the entire world of experience (both actual and imagined) in whatever way I choose to inform and propel the story." –Mark Farrington

"Today I confess that I have made many mistakes, but telling the truth isn't one of them." –Julia Park Tracey

"I think one of the true pleasures of being a writer is the merging of fact and fiction. Perception is everything in our field. Put ten people in the middle of a single event and you'll get ten different stories. How can you

not love that? But with ten versions, where is the truth?"
–Ellen Bryson

"We quibble over genre. I say, let the critics decide what's what. I'm still a kid who loves telling stories, even if sometimes they happen to be true." –Fred A. Wilcox

A final note. My project stalled about a year into compiling stories. Too much paying work demanded my attention; not enough time. Marian Wernicke, my co-editor, joined me this spring and infused the project with new energy. She and the invaluable assistance of Amanda Vacharat brought *Confessions: Fact or Fiction?* to life.

The three of us welcome you to a book dedicated to the art of writing, be it fiction or memoir. We hope you'll enjoy it and suggest it to your friends. We welcome your thoughts and would love for you to post them on our blog: www:chrysaliseditorial.com/blog.

Herta B. Feely
December 2010

My Father's Court

Mark Farrington

THERE WAS A TIME THE BOY STOOD beside his father. Eight years old, ankle-deep in fresh-fallen snow, on the wide concrete step outside the back door of the high school gymnasium. A few straggling snowflakes flitter from an oatmeal sky. The boy's father takes off one glove, pins it in his armpit, and searches the brass key ring attached to his belt, isolating each key and holding it up to the diffused light of the street lamp behind them, because the light above the back door isn't working. "Have to fix that, too," the boy's father says about the bulb. "I'll catch hell from the coach if they have to tromp through here in the dark."

A laugh pops out of him in a cloud of cold air. The same laugh, nervous and childlike, that irritates the boy's mother so. *You won't think it's so funny,* he hears her say, *when you wake up some morning and find me gone.*

Recently, the boy has realized he and his father share the same curly dark hair and green eyes. They both like Abbott and Costello, who the boy's mother calls, *Idiots. A pair of clowns.*

I don't think this is it," the boy's father says about one key, then forces it anyway. "I already tried this one, I think," he says about another. But this one turns, making the lock click free. "Eureka, Watson!" he cries. When he jerks open the door, the warm air pouring out stings the boy's tight cold cheeks. Even his eyebrows feel stiff.

"At least the furnace is working tonight," his father says. The boy follows him upstairs, imagining the horror of an ice-cold gym. "Here we are." The door closes, trapping them in the immense dark.

Lights pop on, a row of them, then another, and the formless dark gives way to a high ceiling and walls, and a floor of pure magic. To the boy it's as gloriously breathtaking as a baseball diamond; more so, because it is a floor and it's been painted – black lines around the edge and more in front of each basket, and in the center a big blue circle with a white "S" in the middle. Superman, the boy thinks, although he knows it stands for Stanton, the high school's name.

"We don't want to cross that line." His father points to the black border, and the boy steps back as if at the edge of a lake during spring thaw. "Not with our boots on, we don't." He laughs. "It's the law."

He unlocks a door in the corner that opens to a closet large as a garage. Inside are rolled-up mats, a folded trampoline. He drops the paper bag he's been carrying onto a card table in front, next to a rack of basketballs, and sits on a folding chair to yank off his boots. The boy tugs his off, too, and when his father picks them up they leave a little puddle of melted snow on the concrete floor.

"You have to wear sneakers to be allowed on the court," his father explains as they put theirs on. Their boots are lined up on top of the newspaper, the large boots and the small boots matching the way the boy and his father would look if they, too, stood side by side.

"Socks would be okay. They used to have sock hops. That's a dance. The kids took off their shoes and danced around the floor in their socks."

He grabs a long-handled dust mop. "You want to shoot baskets?" The boy shakes his head. His father removes his shirt, leaving him in a white tee bunched up in back, where the blue band of his boxer shorts sticks out above the waist of his pants.

As he pushes the dust mop, the floor that already shines, glows even brighter in his wake. There are wide empty lanes on either side of the court, then a single row of bleachers, eight feet high, against each wall. The boy is wondering how people will climb up there when his father puts a key into a hole in the cement-block wall, then grabs the bottom slat and begins to walk backwards, toward the court. The bleachers follow, opening like an accordion, one row and then another, and another above that.

When people start arriving, the boy finds a place on the stage behind one basket, where his father has lined up two rows of chairs. He sits on the end, next to the big red curtain that smells of mildew and dust. His father calls him over to meet the coach. "This is my son, Jay," his father says. "Jay, this is Coach Morelli."

The coach is taller than the boy's father, and muscular, with a weathered face beneath crewcut white hair. His huge calloused hand swallows the boy's.

"Pleased to meet you, Jay." He has a deep voice and a face that seems unable to smile even when he wants to. The boy cannot bring himself to speak.

"I guess we've had enough snow to carry us through the whole winter," the boy's father says.

Suddenly the floor begins to tremble. There's a sound like stampeding horses, and the doors to the locker room burst open and a dozen enormous bodies pour forth, all dressed in blue and white.

All the players seem like giants. The boy has heard of professional players standing seven feet tall, but on television they all look small.

During warm-ups the boy moves to the balcony above the far basket. He likes the perspective of looking down over everything. Beyond where the players shoot lay-ups stands his father, arms folded, chatting to anyone who passes by.

The buzzer sounds in the gym now bloated with heat and noise, and the boy races downstairs, hoping to make it back to the stage before the game begins. Halfway there, he hears the announcer say, "Will everyone please rise for our national anthem." The crowd rises in a single whoosh, and the boy freezes, backing into the people crowding around him, and placing his hand over his heart as a scratching sound fills the air, then the anthem explodes from the loudspeakers.

The moment it ends the boy races for the stage. People clap and stamp their feet. Passing the corner where his father has been standing, the boy spots him in the storage closet, bending over an old record player. He looks up and laughs. "Just call me Harry Phillip Sousa."

The game is close throughout the first half. Stanton's best player is Nate Wiliamson, the only black player on either team, a guard who darts around swiping the ball and racing away like a speedy little kid taunting bullies. The boy favors Tommy Bishop, a muscular forward who always seems to get the rebound. Big for his age and chubby, the boy can easily pretend to be Tommy, who has short dark hair neatly trimmed and a stoic expression whether he's just scored a basket or been called for a foul he didn't commit.

At halftime, his father buys the boy an ice cream sandwich that melts fast in the heat, coating his hands with chocolate and sticky cream. "You'd better go to the men's room and wash up," his father advises, leading him along the narrow trail between the court's black line and the first row of bleachers, saying hello to a half-dozen people along the way. A line stretches out through the propped-open bathroom door. Although relieved when his father leaves him, the boy feels lost in the forest of men.

When he comes out his father is pushing the big dust mop up and down the floor again. He decides to watch the second half from the balcony. Above and behind the basket, he has a clear view of Tommy Bishop muscling rebounds. The game is tense, the other team leading by three points as the fourth quarter begins. The movement and colors and noise and heat all merge together, and leaning over the balcony rail, the boy becomes Tommy Bishop grabbing a rebound, tapping it against the backboard so softly it drops through the hoop, bringing his team within one point with thirty seconds to play. The crowd leaps to its feet, then settles into rhythmic clapping as the other team calls time out.

When play resumes the other team plays keep-away to run out the clock, forcing Nate Williamson to foul their best shooter, a guard.

The lights on the scoreboard above where the boy's father stands read :09. The score is 54-53. The guard has one-and-one, getting the second shot only if he makes the first. Making both will put his team up by three, and there is no three-point shot.

A rumbling rises from every corner of the gym, crescendoing as the guard walks to the free throw line. "Miss it!" the boy screams.

The ball hits the rim, bounces once, and falls off into the sure hands of Tommy Bishop. He whips a pass to Nate Williamson, who slices between two opposing players racing down the court, stops at his favorite spot at the top of the key and goes straight into the air. The boy is perfectly positioned to watch the orange ball rise out of those two black hands, pause at its highest point as if it is a balloon about to float away, then drop through the hoop as the buzzer sounds and the crowd erupts.

The boy jumps up and down. On the court, players and fans mob Nate Williamson.

Later, after the gym has emptied, the boy's father removes his shirt again, lifts the bottom of the lowest bleacher and pushes until that row folds into the one above it, then both into the one above that, until all the bleachers again look like a single bench against the wall, eight feet high. Dust and trash coat the floor the bleachers covered.

Exhausted, the boy sits on the floor by the stage, wishing the players downstairs would finish dressing and leave so his father could take him home.

His father picks up something off the floor. "What do you know?" he says. "A quarter." He holds out his hand. "Here, you have it."

The quarter seems large compared to the nickels and dimes the boy is used to. "Sometimes I make out pretty good going through here," his father says, gesturing toward the trash. "The change falls out of people's pockets. One time I found a five-dollar bill."

This wakes the boy up. "I have to put the bleachers up on the other side," his father says. "If you want to look around here while I'm doing that, you can keep whatever you find."

His words transform the trash heap into a treasure trove the boy searches methodically, unearthing another quarter, two dimes, and seven pennies.

"Now try the other side," his father instructs. "That side's where the visiting team's fans sit, so usually there are more adults." He laughs. "Adults have more money to lose than kids."

The dollar bill the boy finds, folded up beneath a cup, proves his father's words true. The boy will be a father himself, his own father gone, before he considers that his father might have planted it.

That night, he clutches the money in his sweaty palm, dreaming of baseball cards, midget race cars, Pez. Overcome by fatigue once again, he pushes the money carefully into his pants pocket and sits in the chair his father has taken down off the stage. "It won't be long now," his father says.

When the door opens, the boy jerks out of the sleep he's been tumbling into. Not five feet away, his shiny dark hair slicked back, a gym bag slung over one shoulder, stands Tommy Bishop. He wears a blue and white letterman's jacket with a football on the front, and snow boots nearly to his knees.

Nate Williamson follows him, wearing a gray rain coat that doesn't look warm enough for the winter, gray dress pants, and shiny black shoes.

"Drained that sucker, stopped on a dime." Nate's voice has a lilt like poetry.

The boy's father, scraping some gum stuck to the floor beneath the bleachers, calls, "Hey, boys."

"Hey, Skinner," Nate replies. The boy does not know what the nickname means, but it does not sound complimentary.

"Good game tonight, boys."

Tommy Bishop grabs a ball off the rack and flips it to Nate. "Show us the touch."

As Nate drops his bag and bounces the ball, the boy's father calls good-naturedly, "No shoes on the court, boys."

Nate ignores him. "You get under the basket," he tells Tommy. "Snatch that rebound and feed me the outlet pass."

"Come on, boys." His father has risen to his feet. "We don't want to damage the floor."

When Tommy tries to flip the ball off the rim, it goes through the hoop instead. "You got to miss, man. You got to miss so I can make my shot."

"Come on, boys," the boy's father says again.

Tommy shoots and misses, but the ball skirts from his grasp and dribbles toward the boy's feet. He bends down and picks it up.

This next the boy will remember all his life. Tommy has taken several steps in his direction. Hands extended, he nods for the ball. Beneath his still-damp hair, there's a squareness to his jaw and the promise of something simple and honest in his brown eyes. In the distance beyond Tommy's shoulder stands the boy's father. His baggy pants sag beneath the bulge of his belly. Pale bony shoulders, weak red face. The stick of the mop he holds rises taller than he is.

The boy will be unable to recall the emotion in his father's face. Understanding? Gentle forgiveness? His father was that kind of man. Or did he feel it like a knife the boy's hands pushed forward, instead of the ball that curled into the air, pausing at its highest point as if it were a balloon about to float away, before settling into the hands of Tommy Bishop, who spun and whipped a pass to the already running Nate Williamson?

Nate caught the ball like a wide receiver, dribbled once to gain his balance, and rose into the air. The ball soared from his hand, clanked the rim, and dropped harmlessly to one side.

"Shit," Nate hisses. Landing, his heel gashes a long black streak in the floor.

"That's all right," Tommy consoles. "You hit that shot when it counted."

"You got that right."

Nate grabs his bag. They button up their coats in preparation for the cold. "Take it easy, Skinner," Nate calls. "Little Skinner, too."

Cold air rushes in when they open the door. The boy's father laughs. "They're pretty excited about the game." He walks to the top of the key to inspect the damage done by Nate's shoes.

The boy waits in silence, thoughts turned to his mother sitting glumly in front of the television at home, while his father on hands and knees scrubs those marks with steel wool.

φ

CATCHING ATOMS

R. Dean Johnson

THE FIRST DAY OF SCHOOL AND IT'S ONE OF THOSE cold ones where the sky looks like it came right out of a black-and-white movie. We're still unpacking, and the box with all my jackets is who knows where. So it's either my winter coat, which even I know would look ridiculous in California, or my dad's old work jacket—a navy blue, sharp-collared,   cut-tight-at-the-bottom-so-it-doesn't-get-sucked-into-machinery, machinist's jacket. I go with the work jacket even though it fits all saggy in the shoulders and so long in the sleeves I have to cuff them just so my hands can make it out far enough to carry my backpack. And on top of all that, there's a patch over the heart with my dad's nickname on it, "Packy."

My mom says it'll be okay, that making new friends will be tough for my little brother and sister too. But Brendan and Colleen are still in grade school, and little kids don't care what you're wearing or how you do your hair. Not like junior high, where everybody notices everything. Especially when you're new. That's why it would be a lot easier if I had my Paterson All-Stars jacket, because then the guys would all see I can play ball, and they'd probably like me right away.

When I get to school, I don't stuff the jacket in my locker like I would have back home. In southern California, everything is outside. Instead of hallways, there are breezeways, which is a nice way of saying tunnel. And you might not think it can get all that cold in California, but on a cloudy day you can keep ice cream from melting in one of those breezeways.

Right before lunch, this guy comes up to my locker and says, "Hey Packy, where you from?"

He isn't real big, but he's bigger than me, so I try to be cool about it. "Jersey."

"Jersey?" he says. "Isn't New Jersey where all the fags hang out?"

"You'd know," I say.

It's barely out of my mouth before he's got me by the collar of my jacket. "I know only a faggot would wear a jacket like this."

People around the lockers stop what they're doing and look at me like maybe I'm supposed to have some big reaction. Then someone behind me says in a real casual voice, "Knock it off, Jaime."

As this Jaime guy lets my collar go and steps back, some big guy with his hair perfectly combed so it looks kind of messed up steps around me. His shirt is this nerdy, checkered button-up that's hanging out everywhere except by the back pocket where his yellow, Velcro wallet is sticking out. You can tell it's that way on purpose, like a gun holster, like he could whip out his money real fast in case of an emergency.

He looks around at everybody, then says, "How you doing? I'm Garrett." He reaches out and flicks the patch on my jacket." Is your name really Packy?"

"Nah. It's Reece."

"Reece?" he says." What kind of name is that?"

Everybody laughs and I'm thinking maybe he's setting me up. "The kind my dad would give me, I guess."

Garrett gets this smirk and looks me over. "Cool jacket, man."

"You busting my chops?"

"Busting your chops?" He glances around like maybe Jaime or somebody can explain what that means, only nobody says anything." You mean razzin' you?"

"Yeah, I guess."

"No, man. It's Fonzie cool."

"Yeah?" I say, looking around to see who's grinning and about to laugh at me. "I think it's about that old, too."

"Maybe," he says and laughs, and when Garrett laughs, everybody else starts laughing. "You're quick," he says. "You should hang with us."

"Totally," Jaime says and slaps my shoulder the way your buddies do when you make a great catch. "Sit at our table for lunch, Reece."

That's all it takes and I'm one of the guys. But just to be safe, I wear my dad's jacket to school every day.

*

Looking at Clifford Matlin, you'd think he could be one of the guys too. He's as big as Garrett, but he doesn't know how to use it for sports or anything. All it does is make him easier to spot in a crowd and see how weird he is. You see his head over everyone else's at assemblies, his hair hanging down in his eyes and every two seconds him pushing it over the rim of his glasses or tucking it behind his ears. Sometimes, he shows up to school wearing jeans that are too long and cuffed like it's the fifties. Other times, he wears this big, fluffy, turtleneck sweater with a patch that says, *1980 Olympic Winter Games, Lake Placid.* The patch is cool, you know, kind of sporty, but everyone makes fun of the sweater because who wears turtlenecks in Southern California? And no matter how hot it is, he's always got this red windbreaker with him, sometimes on, sometimes tied around his waist or stuffed in his backpack, but always there, like his mom won't let him out of the house without it.

One day, Clifford brings this glass jar to Pre-Algebra and hunches over it the whole time with both hands on the lid. Every couple of minutes he reaches a hand out into the air and pinches his fingers together like he's caught something. Then he unscrews the lid of the jar, flicks whatever it is inside, and screws the lid back on. When I ask him what he's doing he whispers, "Catching atoms for an experiment." Then he grins like it's some funny joke.

I don't razz Clifford or anything when he tells me. Who is it going to hurt if he catches a few atoms? That doesn't stop other people though. The girl in front of me starts telling everyone around us and in five minutes you can see people on the other side of the room whispering and then looking over at Clifford and giggling. By the time the bell rings, he looks kind of mad and mumbles something about Albert Einstein's teachers not understanding his genius. "Maybe his accent was too thick," somebody says, and a bunch of people laugh. Then they tell the people who haven't heard, and before you know it everyone is laughing their way out the door and not listening to a thing Clifford says.

At lunch, Jaime can't stop looking around for Clifford, wanting to see if he still has the jar. I try to act like that's stupid and we should play basketball or something like we always do, but when the guys spot Clifford sitting over by the tennis courts with the jar right next to him in the grass, they take off to razz him. And it's not like I join in or anything. I just hang back and watch him take it until Garrett says to back off because it's too easy, and what's the point of that?

*

When baseball season starts, I get drafted on to Garrett's team — the best team in the league. Our coach tells us second place is just a coward's way to say you lost, and he swears he'll bench anyone, even Garrett, if you miss practice for anything besides dying. But that's okay, because we can't get enough baseball. Every day at lunch Garrett gets some guys together to play pickle, and since I'm on his team, I'm always one of the guys.

About a week before summer vacation, we're playing pickle and Jaime launches the ball past me like a missile. It skips across the grass all the way over to the fence by the tennis courts. I run after it, and as I get closer I see the ball has wiped out Clifford's apple juice. He's got the ball in his hand, staring at it like it's a meteorite or something. Then he looks at me through his hair, his eyes squinty because of the sun. "I think you owe me an apple juice."

I say, "Sorry, it was an accident."

He shakes his head no and grips the ball with both hands. Everyone is waiting, so I tell him, "It's not even my ball, Cliff. It's Jaime's. If you don't give it back, he's going to get pretty mad."

Clifford ignores me and stuffs the ball in his backpack, his windbreaker all around it like a nest. He zips everything up, and just like that all the guys come over.

Jaime gets in Clifford's face, and just as he's about to rip the backpack away Garrett stops him. Garrett doesn't stick his hand out or anything; he just says, "Come on, Clifford, lunch is almost over. Give us the ball."

Clifford stares at the grass, shakes his head and mumbles, "N-no."

People who weren't even playing start coming over then, everyone making this half circle behind Garrett. Garrett asks Clifford for the ball again and gets another no, and you might think he's expecting that the way he lets his head drop slow and relaxed, bobbing a little on the way down, almost like he's nodding. He stares at the spot in the grass Clifford's staring at, then raises his head back up. "You're gonna need to give that back, Cliff. Unless you're feeling lucky." Garrett crosses his arms, and they look kind of big all coiled together. "You feeling lucky, Cliff?"

We all laugh and Garrett could let it die right there, but he has the crowd. "If you can't see a ball rolling toward you, those glasses aren't doing you much good. Maybe you need a haircut. Or a guide dog."

Everybody busts up at that, even me, but it doesn't matter. Clifford still has the ball in his backpack and both hands wrapped around one of the straps. And without looking at anyone except Garrett, he says as clear as anything, "At least I don't use a pound of grease to keep my hair out of my eyes."

It's not exactly the best comeback ever, but Garrett looks pretty shocked anything came out of Clifford's mouth. "Give me the ball, Clifford. Give me the ball right now, man, say you're sorry for that little comment, and you'll get to keep existing."

Clifford shakes his head and pulls tighter on the straps of his backpack.

"Poor guy's having a meltdown," Garrett says, except nobody's laughing anymore. So with his finger an inch from Clifford's nose, Garrett says, "If you don't want to spend the rest of your life dead, you'll give me that ball right now."

"No."

"I don't want to have to fight you over this, man."

Clifford looks around at everybody and says, "Why? Are you scared of me?"

Garrett isn't scared. He can't be. But it seems like forever before he finally throws up his hands and says, "Fine, today after school. Behind the bleachers." His face is glowing, and he looks Clifford over one more time. "You better be ready," he says, then walks away.

*

Everyone runs out to the far edge of the football field as soon as school lets out. I'm one of the first people around the backside of the bleachers, and Clifford is there just like he said he'd be. In about a minute, a circle two or three people deep forms around him and a bunch of other people climb to the top of the bleachers to look over the back.

When Garrett finally slips through the crowd, he slaps my shoulder and says, "This will probably only take a second." He looks at me real confident, then tosses his backpack to Jaime and steps inside the circle.

Garrett lets it quiet down, looking around and taking in all the faces before stopping at Clifford's. "This is your last chance, man. Just give me the ball, say you're sorry, and we'll be cool. You won't get hurt."

Clifford stands there, his face totally blank and his hands hanging by his sides, all bunched up into fists. He stares straight ahead into nothing, and you can't tell if he's even listening.

"Well," Garrett shakes his head, "at least take off your glasses."

Clifford snatches his glasses with one hand and tosses them backwards without looking. It's amazing because the glasses don't crash down in the grass like you'd expect; they land on top of his backpack all gentle—as if he planned it that way. The one thing Clifford ever got right, and he doesn't even notice. He walks to the middle of the circle, stops, tucks some hair behind his ears, bends his knees, and brings his fists up near his eyes the way guys on TV do. It looks ridiculous because you know the only way a guy's going to win a fight with a stance like that is if he's the star of the show.

Garrett shuffles forward, steady, and puts his fists out in front of his chest. I've never seen him fight, but he sure looks like he knows what he's doing. Everyone starts cheering, calling out Garrett's name and rooting him on. But me, I don't make a sound; I just push forward a little and get on my tiptoes to see everything.

They start circling each other, waiting to see who's going to throw the first punch. Garrett looks sharp, the way you'd expect, but Clifford doesn't look scared like you might think, just focused. Then Garrett swings low, splitting Clifford's arms and catching him square in the stomach. Clifford's eyes open real wide, like he's surprised, and his hands drop. He winds up to counter-punch, but Garrett connects solid on his cheek, and he falls.

The circle explodes in cheers and guys like Jaime Muzi pump their fist the way you do when a guy hits a homerun. We all know it's over because Clifford doesn't try to get up. He just lays there, doubled-over on the ground. Garrett waits a few seconds, to make sure, then he goes over to Clifford's backpack and pulls the ball out. Half of Clifford's jacket comes out too, like it didn't want to let go, and his glasses fall to the side. You might think Garret would hold the ball up all victorious, but he just sets Clifford's glasses back on top of the backpack, then walks to the edge of the circle real fast, tosses the ball to Jaime, and keeps going right through the crowd. Everyone goes after him and slaps him on the back and congratulates him like he's some kind of hero.

I wait to see if Clifford will get up, and after the last few people clear out, he does. He's holding his stomach as he walks over to gather up his stuff, and when he kneels down I see the tears streaming from his eyes. But he isn't crying. He just pulls his jacket all the way out and wipes his face with the soft, cotton part in the lining. And though you can already see the red mark where Garrett connected, Clifford doesn't make a sound. It takes him both hands to fit his glasses over his ears and then he looks up at me through that stupid hair. I want to say something, to tell him it was a good try or a lucky punch, but all I do is stare at him a few seconds until I hear someone calling my name.

I step out from behind the bleachers and Garrett's halfway across the field now, stopped and looking back for me. We're teammates, so I guess he's wondering why I'm not there congratulating him like everyone else. He calls my name again and it sounds like a question, "Reece?" All the other people shut up then and stare. I look back at Clifford who's standing now, a few feet away. I really want to say something, but I know I have the crowd, so I reach my hand out a little ways, pinch my fingers together like I've caught an atom, and put it in my pocket. From so far away, I figure no one else can see that, but as I take off to catch up to Garrett, a few people cheer like it's the best joke ever. Like I've razzed Clifford. I don't know if Clifford understands that I don't mean it like that; I just know I've got to leave him standing there all alone.

φ

THE TATTLETALE
Marian O'Shea Wernicke

M Y COUSIN JOE HAS BEEN DEAD FOR YEARS NOW, but I sometimes wish I could talk to him about a certain summer and ask him if I really ruined his life.

Several summers in a row when I was between eight and ten years old, I spent a week at my aunt and uncle's house in north St. Louis. This visit was a treat for me on several fronts. As the oldest of seven children growing up in a big noisy house thirty-five miles west of St. Louis, my world was one of three circles of houses--substantial two story houses that had belonged to army officers during World War II, each with its own acre of unfenced yard bordered by woods, fields, and a pond where we went ice-skating in the winter, with the nearest general store a long hot bike-ride away. Our parents were all city people who found this idyllic roomy place perfect for raising their ever-larger broods of kids. This was the 50's, and many of them were good Catholics--hoping Pope Pius XII would change his mind about birth control, but still loyal to the rules. When we went to the nearby St. Joseph's School in Cottleville, the farm kids saw us as city slickers, but we knew we were country kids compared to our city cousins.

So the invitation to spend a week in town was alluring, and I made my little brothers and sisters jealous with tales of traffic noise, hot pavements, and a corner drug store I could walk to every day for my ration of Juicy Fruit gum and Hershey bars. Aunt Helen, my mother's older sister, was a big, soft, plump woman with an easy laugh who adored me. She had married a man from the neighborhood, and Uncle Al was a gentle, hard-working meat-packer who nursed a Budweiser after work every day and tolerated my chatty presence. My two cousins, Nancy and Joe, were much older than I, already out of high school and working. Nancy treated me like a favorite pet, and I relished the spoiling I didn't get at home from my busy, often pregnant mother. To me, Nancy was the height of glamour as she ran off to catch the bus for her sales job at a downtown department store, her reddish-blond pageboy swinging, her lips scarlet, and her high heels clipping down the front steps. Joe, who mostly ignored me, was a tall, handsome guy in his early twenties, always rushing out to play ball or pick up his fiancée, Sue.

One hot July night during one of these visits, when the locusts were buzzing in the tall elm trees that lined Marcus Avenue, Aunt Helen asked Joe to keep an eye on me while she went to St. Englebert's to play bingo. Uncle Al was already snoring in their stifling downstairs bedroom. I saw Joe wince, and heard him mutter, "Aw, Mom! Steve and I had plans tonight."

"Don't worry," I piped up. "I'll sit in the back seat and be quiet as a mouse." Joe groaned. We dropped Aunt Helen off at church, and soon Joe and I were on our way down the street in his old blue Chevy to pick up Steve. The guys sat in front smoking, their white t-shirts rolled up high on tanned, muscular arms, cigarettes propped rakishly behind their ears. I was in heaven. Only ten and out with two guys who looked and sounded like James Dean! I hunched forward on the sticky vinyl back seat, my dirty red Keds propped on the hump in the floor and listened. Through the open windows came the whoosh of passing cars and the sticky sweet smell of a St. Louis summer night.

Their conversation was desultory at first, low murmurs lost in the passing traffic. Suddenly, Joe's voice rose in exasperation.

"I've just about had it with Sue. She's been a real drag lately. Never wants to do anything I want to do." He glanced at Steve, who was absently nodding his head to Bill Haley's *Shake, Rattle and Roll.* "She hates my friends, too."

Steve nodded sympathetically and took a drag off his cigarette. "Man, she even wants me to take her to the Muny Opera next week!" They snorted with laughter and dragged in unison on their Camel cigarettes. The next part I missed as they murmured and then exploded with sudden guffaws.

Stunned, I sat back in the cavernous seat. Hot humid air blew my hair across my face. How could Joe talk like that about Sue? They were engaged to be married! I worshiped Sue's cool blond perfection. Her father was a doctor, and although their house was only a few blocks away, it was a world away from the small red brick house of my aunt and uncle. Suddenly a plan formed in my busy brain. I would pay Sue a visit the next day and warn her. She was about to lose Joe.

That night in bed I rehearsed my story. I'd leave out the snorting laughter, but I'd make her see that Joe might be slipping away. Maybe she could change, start asking to go see the Cardinals game instead of the Muny. Dressed in my blue church dress, white anklets and black patent leather shoes, I paid Sue a visit the next day. She ushered me into the living room of her parents' solid two story house, and I had a fleeting sense of dark coolness, silky beige furniture, a soft rose carpet, everything hushed and dim, shuttered against the noonday glare.

What I can't remember is our conversation, but I do recall the quiet way she sat on the edge of the sofa, and listened to the story of last night's ride. Finally, Sue walked me to the door and when she bent down to kiss me, I could smell something like lilacs. Did I imagine it, or were there tears in her eyes?

*

The dull pain in my stomach didn't begin until dinner that night as we all sat down around the table in the hot kitchen. No fan, no air conditioning. Finally by dessert, I thought I'd throw up. I stared at my fast melting ice cream. I knew I had to say something, I just didn't know what.

"Joe," I began.

Distractedly he lowered the sports page of *The St. Louis Post-Dispatch.* "Yeah?"

Then the words sputtered out of me. "I went over to Sue's today."

His eyes narrowed as they focused on me. "What'd you two talk about?"

"Oh, I just told her some stuff you and Steve were talking about last night in the car--" I waited. He said nothing at first, then lowered his face into his hands. I tried smiling at him, but my lips trembled.

Then he shoved his chair back and shot me a murderous glance. "Damn it, Miss Big Mouth!"

He grabbed his keys, and the screen door slammed behind him, scaring Aunt Helen so much she dropped the casserole she was clearing from the table. They all stared at me as the Chevy screeched away from the curb.

I've tried to imagine that scene between Joe and Sue many times, but all I know is that they broke off their engagement that night. I heard the grownups whispering about it for weeks. Joe didn't speak to me for several years. Not even at Grandma's house on Christmas day. I never did learn what happened to Sue. I imagine her today living in one of the posh houses in the Central West End, wearing a cashmere twin set and walking her grandchildren to St. Roch's school. A few years later, Joe married an earthy, good-natured gal named Betty. They had four little boys by the time Joe died of cancer at age thirty-nine.

Joe, the locusts are still singing on hot summer nights, but the elms have died. Your sons grew up to be strong and handsome, and I've lost count of your grandchildren. Betty comes to the annual family reunion, and when she hugs me I think of you. I wish we could sit down on a bench, then, in the stillness of evening in the park, I could say what I never could say, that I'm sorry, that I was a foolish little girl, and that I hope you've forgiven me for being a tattletale.

φ

OVER THE FALLS
Tim Wendel

CLOSER TO THE PRECIPICE, *the river's surface becomes white-mad with froth. It surges past Goat and Three Sisters islands, past the Luna islet, which divides the American cataract. Then the mighty river pitches briefly out and downward into the eternal basin, the land where tourists in yellow-colored rain slickers glimpse the roiling waters and chatter excitedly about the wonder of it all.*

Father Hennepin was the first white man to gaze upon this sight. When he saw the towering clouds of mist and heard the river's thunder, he grew fearful of the Niagara River's "mesmerizing effect." The onrushing waters seemed to beckon to him. Called for the good father to walk into the waters and be carried toward what? Heaven or hell? In the shadow of the Niagara, Hennepin took down the portable altar he carried on his back and knelt to pray. He prayed to be spared.

What Hennepin and the others who followed him discovered is that the thirty-five-mile-long Niagara is the greatest "short" river in the world. In the rapids above the Falls, it reaches speeds of twenty-five miles per hour. After falling nearly two hundred feet at the Falls itself, the current has been clocked at thirty miles per hour as it flows through the Devil's Hole Rapids.

In the last few miles of its life, before the Niagara River empties into Lake Ontario, the current still runs fast, nearly five knots. Sailboats are moored to orange balloon buoys. They belong to the rich ones from the Falls, Tonawanda and Porterville. The crafts hug the shallows in the small coves along the shore, with their bows pointed upriver, as if in quiet homage.

*

"Russell, you're killing me." I grumble.

He's supposed to be writing about French Lick, Indiana -- not about the Niagara River and Western New York. The last time Russell and I spoke was when I flew up for the photo shoot in Cooperstown. There, over a quick lunch, he asked if he could send along portions of a novel he was working on and like an idiot I agreed. Now that's all he seems to be sending me. It doesn't matter if his descriptions of the land where we grew up are dead on because any good magazine, especially a sports magazine, doesn't deal with reality as much as people would like to think. We offer up illusions and attitudes and lifestyle. That and sports and photos of scantily clad women. That's what sells magazines to men.

"Not exactly what you were hoping for, is it?" Jen says.

My assistant stands in the doorway, giving me that killer smile of hers.

"What do you think?" I say.

"I think we've got to scramble if this is going to make the new issue," she says. I find it interesting how she says we. "In last week's we said the next installment would be about French Lick, the home of Larry Bird."

"You've read this?"

"He CC'd both of us."

Beautiful, I think to myself, now she knows it has nothing to do with what we've promised. Jen remains in the door, watching me sweat. She's dressed in a dark skirt with an off-white shirt that's unbuttoned to reveal her regal white neck and a hint of cleavage. My assistant has blonde hair with the occasional highlight, cut shoulder-length so she's able to brush it behind an ear. That's a nervous habit she has. About the only one I've seen so far because Jen is as sharp as they come.

"So, we need to pull together what we can about French Lick."

"I already have," she says.

"Good, start sending me some background. I was in French Lick years ago for the *Examiner*."

"I found that piece, too."

I raise my eyebrows. "What? You reading my mind again? That can be dangerous."

Jen just smiles.

"All right, I've got to meet with our esteemed publisher this morning. I'll start working this and then we'll tag-team it."

"Does his byline stay on it?"

I should have seen this coming. Jen is so ambitious.

"It's Russell's byline for now," I say and watch as she purses her lips, faking a pout. "But don't worry. We'll get you on a story worth shouting about soon."

She smiles one last time and returns to her desk.

I have forty-five minutes before the editorial meeting. The weekly gathering where our publisher, Robbie Slater, tells us what kind of stories we should be doing and regales us with the hard lessons of life.

"French Lick, French Lick," I repeat to myself, trying to recall anything from my only visit to that town. It was soon after Larry Bird retired and rumor had it he was in town, but I never saw him. Not that it mattered. For a man is a reflection of where he grew up. That's what we want to believe. That Abraham Lincoln was such a fine man because he split logs in Illinois. That Harry Truman was as honest and as predictable as the wide Kansas prairie. That Larry Bird could shoot a basketball with such a sweet arc because he grew up in a place as sweet-sounding as French Lick, Indiana.

I'm not sure if any of that is true anymore. But it makes for a good story, and from where I sit, editing one of the top men's magazines at the tender age of twenty-nine, I need good stories. I need to tap into the reader's sense of righteousness and delusions of grandeur.

"French Lick will always be shabby around the edges," I write. "Reminiscent of a more innocent time. A painting drawn by Thornton Wilder or Edward Hopper."

Not bad. Not bad at all.

I look down upon 42nd Street. Our offices are twenty stories up, across from Grand Central, and the morning rush is about over. With their briefcases, backpacks, overstuffed athletic bags, the commuters could be refugees fleeing some distant conflagration. They believe that their days are laid out for them when, of course, they know nothing of how it will be. None of us do. To watch the commuters returning for another day, to lean back in my swivel chair and peer down from my office window I like to pretend I can read their minds. Sometimes my eyes will follow one of them for as long as I can, nearly three blocks, until that instant when they fall from sight. The more minds that I can read, the longer I can stay in power. It's as simple as that, and I intend to be here for a long time.

One of my outside lines rings and Jen picks it up.

"Mrs. Shelby Walton," she calls in. Now this is a surprise. I was planning to call her this morning, before the crisis about French Lick outflanked me.

"How are you, Shelby?" I say and for a moment I'm greeted with nothing but silence on the other end.

Then, finally, "Garrett, are you there?"

"Of course I am."

Then the first of the pauses, the forecasted lulls in our conversation, begins. For this is often the way Shelby and I carry on. So much lies buried beneath our dialogue. An entire story that we both know by heart. When we were in high school, I tried to fill such times with my nervous words. Now I've come to understand that such pauses can be as precious as anything we truly tell each other. For I know that I must bite my tongue. It's the only way. For this woman moves to her own music and all I can do is follow.

"Have you heard from Russell?" she asks. "The other night you said that today was his next deadline."

"He sent me something. Something I can't really use because it's not about what I asked him to write."

"But have you talked to him?"

"No, I haven't talked to him since last week when I saw him in up Cooperstown. We changed the logo on the package. We have him posing in front of the Thunderbird we got for him."

"I've seen it," Shelby says and a hint of irritation creeps into her voice. "But you haven't really talked to him?"

"No, Shel, I haven't."

Together we fall into another pause and I can almost hear her sigh of disappointment.

"When this started he promised to call Deb-Deb every day. Now he hasn't called since last weekend."

Now it's my turn to grow quiet. For how do I explain all of this? That Russell was sent away so we could share more moments, more pauses, like this one.

"The people here really like the series," I say. "It's gained energy all of its own. I'm sorry, but he maybe gone for awhile longer."

Here comes another pause. A long, sweet one.

"All right," she murmurs.

*

Now I know what you're thinking. How could I do this? Russell was one of my best friends in high school. I know what I've put in motion is wrong, maybe immoral. When Russell and Shelby were married I was in the wedding party, of course. The second one to raise a glass in their honor at the reception afterward.

Still, we like to think that the major decisions in a life -- where to go to school, what profession to follow, whom to marry -- are always tied to logic and reason. But you and I both know they rarely are. So often the crucial points in a life come down to a glance, just the right word, a feeling that this is the way. It's the small moments that propel us in a particular direction.

For too long I've pushed ahead in the belief that what's next will be better. That it will somehow heal me. Now I see that the answer lies somewhere in my past, so I must return to our small town on the banks of the Niagara River. I return to woo her, to court her, and to see if time is as fluid, as malleable, as some contend.

φ

LOSING MY RELIGION
Amy Fries

A T SOME POINT, I QUIT BELIEVING in the religion of my birth. In religion, period. A break that left my parents feeling scorned and rejected. "What did we do wrong?" my mother still asks. "It's-not-you-it's-me," I defend myself with that old but true standby. After all, faith cannot be faked.

Time and again, when I try to pinpoint the beginnings of my long struggle between doubt and faith, I find myself back in Sister Anna Marie's piano room in the convent of the Blessed Sacrament, the room with the green vinyl couch, the brown-and-white checkered asbestos-tile floor, the walls barren, except of course, for the omnipresent 3-D crucifix. No sleek modern symbols here. This was the body of Christ, nailed in twisted pain onto the cross. The room reeked with the stench of a disinfectant that novice nuns regularly swabbed all over the convent. The decor, I'm sure, was supposed to inspire quiet reflection, but for me, it inspired terror, terror of falling short of the judgment of Sister Anna Marie.

But the most outstanding piece in the room was the piano itself. Plastic wrap covered the entire upright except for the keys. That way Sister Anna Marie could protect it from the grubby fingerprints of her halfhearted charges.

I had taken lessons from Sister Anna Marie, from 1968 through 1972, third grade through the eighth. She looked ancient to me back then, though she was probably only in her seventies. She was tall and lean. Bits of gray hair poked out along the edges of her wimple. Vatican II, the document freeing Catholics from the mysteries of Latin and black cloth among others, had occurred in the mid-sixties, and nuns were free to doff the head-to-toe garb. But not Sister Anna Marie. She was too old, I suppose, to change her habits. So she remained with the starched white wimple pinched about her face.

Sister Anna Marie was a dictatorial terror, hovering over the metronome that clicked, clicked, clicked away the nanoseconds of my half-hour lessons. If I failed to tinkle the ivories to the beat, her hands would clap in my face, her foot would stomp on the linoleum until my heartbeat, the metronome, the clapping, and the chords melted into one monstrous internal melody.

Sister Anna Marie had a cluster of warts on her tongue. During my lessons, she sucked on ice cubes she kept in a glass near the piano. One day the ice was down to three well-sucked cubes, melted into small ovals. I was having trouble keeping up with the metronome that day, missing more than the usual number of notes. She asked me what was wrong, and I made the mistake of telling her I had a sore throat.

"Here," she said handing me her glass, "suck on these."

I took the plain glass in my hand, everything of course being plain and utilitarian in the convent, and looked long and hard at those wilted slivers. Then I titled the glass, slid those ice cubes into my mouth, and sucked on them, just as Sister Anna Marie had ordered.

Even as I sat with the ice slivers in my mouth, I couldn't believe that I had acquiesced. I could have just said "no thank you." Why didn't I? It wasn't just because I knew that kids who annoyed Sister Anna Marie were chased out of the room with Sister two steps behind them throwing sheet music at their heads. I believe I sucked on those ice cubes simply because the idea of questioning, even a suggestion, was beyond my imagination.

But Sister Anna Marie had another side too. She had a passion that she did not hide. Occasionally, Sister Anna Marie would take over the piano bench herself, shoving me aside and throwing back the wide sleeves of her habit. And she'd start playing Beethoven or Bach the way they should be played, sometimes with wild abandon, sometimes with a haunting, quiet grace. When she would take over a piece this way, when she would make me forget all the missed notes, the sloppy chords, the fuzzy pedal, when she would lean her body toward the keys, her eyes closed, her face up to God or whatever she believed in at that moment, I thought Sister Anna Marie the finest pianist I had ever encountered.

Who is this woman? I would wonder. How did this feisty person end up hiding beneath voluminous black, with three-foot-long rosary beads for a belt, and a wedding ring that marked her as a bride of Christ?

Many of the nuns seemed so miserable I couldn't believe that they had willingly chosen this life. I wanted to push back the great veil of secrecy and know the truth of their lives. But again, as with the ice cubes, I couldn't break through the barrier.

Wondering about Sister Anna Marie and the others and questioning my blind obedience to them, I see now as the first seeds of my doubt.

After an eight-year-stint in Catholic school, I did make the risky move in 1973 to the public domain. I thought I was forever free of the sterile convent, but no. At fourteen, just a year later, I found myself back in Sister Anna Marie's piano room to attend CCD (Confraternity of Christian Doctrine) classes for those no longer receiving religious instruction on a daily basis.

Sister Peter Damien and Sister Luke presided. They were the hip nuns, the post-Vatican II nuns. Instead of the black habits they wore plaid, itchy wool suits.

Twelve of us, ranging in age from thirteen to sixteen, sat sulking in Sister Anna Marie's piano room for our first CCD class. In my view, I had seen behind the Great Oz's curtain and found that parents and teachers offered nothing that applied to the realities of teenage life—a new world filled with the challenges of sex, drugs, boredom, and cruelty.

But before me now in CCD class was a new type of nun, at least for our small, steel-mill town in western Pennsylvania. To my great surprise, Sister Peter Damien was a pretty twenty-something woman with short, fashionably cut black hair. More amazingly, she was asking for our opinions. "What do you kids want to talk about today?" she said. "Really, ask anything you want."

In response, we stared at the brown-and-white floor, at the crucifix, at the plastic-wrapped piano. We figured the question was a trap.

"Anything," Sister Peter Damien coaxed. With her street clothes and inviting smile, she was a complete novelty for those of us used to more mystical authorities. Finally, her good cheekbones and flawless complexion loosened me up. I volunteered.

"Yes, Amy."

"Is there really a God?" I asked, feeling bold, adult, energized at the idea that we might actually have a free-flowing discussion.

Sister Damien gasped. "We can't talk about that! That's not a point of discussion. Of course there is a God!"

Oh.

That was the last question I ever asked in CCD.

Though I had been temporarily silenced, I have followed the long fault line of doubt ever since I uttered those words in a convent so many years ago. Yet I find, even today, that something about expressing doubt remains a dangerous proposition, a don't-ask, don't-tell notion, a deep, dark secret better not discussed.

So naturally — as a writer and quester — I gravitate toward it.

To steal an often-quoted line from the Catholic theology of probabilism: *ubi dubium, ibi libertas*. Where there is doubt, there is freedom.

*

True Confessions

For many years prior to voicing that question — Is there a God? — I had been a devout elementary school student. "Let the little children come to me, and do not hinder them, for the kingdom of God belongs to such as these." (Luke 18:16)

And come to Him I did. Like every second grader in Sister Cecilia's class, I raised my arm eagerly every time we were asked: "Who wants to be a nun or a priest when they grow up?"

"I do, I do!" we all shouted.

In fact, that year I had announced proudly before the class that when I grew up, I wanted to be either "a nun or a cat burglar."

In elementary school, I was seduced by many aspects of religion, by the kind, loving images of Jesus, Mary, and guardian angels; by the majesty, ritual, and drama of the mass; and by the church with its stained-glass windows, incense, and statues of benevolent saints there to protect me. My connection with God was real as I lifted my face and sang the words of the popular sixties' hymn: "Eat his body, drink his blood, and we'll sing a song of love. Hallelujah."

I was such an obedient, unquestioning soul in those days that when I was eleven years old, I bravely marched to the confessional, knelt on the red pad of the kneeler and forced myself to say, "Bless me father, for I have sinned. I have committed adultery."

Of course, I had no idea what adultery was, but that previous Sunday, Father had urged those who had wandered to go to confession and seek forgiveness for the sin of adultery. And so I did.

Father now sat on the other side of the confessional in silence, stunned I'm sure. He finally responded: "In thought, word, or deed?"

Now this really threw me. Not knowing what adultery was, I could hardly tell if I did it in thought, word, or deed. But thought seemed the safest bet.

"Thought," I said after a moment.

"Oh." I could hear the relief in his voice. "Say six Hail Mary's and don't do it again."

I left the confessional, but I did not feel the lightness of a soul unblemished. I suspected instead that I had been had, that I had been an idiot, like the time I sucked on those ice cubes.

Not long afterward, upon entering public school, I became a semi-rebellious teen (just as Sister Anna Marie had feared). My friends and I went to church begrudgingly. We begged, pleaded, stonewalled, lied — anything — to avoid the CCD classes that doubled the amount of time we had to give up on a Sunday.

My lackluster attitude disappointed my father. He loved the Catholic Church, the formality of it, the rules and regulations, its definite sense of right and wrong. He wanted us to move to another house, a less attractive house in every way, solely so we could be within walking distance of our church — Blessed Sacrament — where he sang in the choir and served on the membership committee. He counted priests and nuns among his best friends, and they sometimes joined us, to my dismay, for Sunday lasagna dinners.

After Vatican II liberalized church rules, the priests of Blessed Sacrament Church selected my father to be one of the few laymen who administered communion on the steps leading to the altar. His hands shook violently when he dispensed the host. My friends would ask me what was wrong with him. On the one hand, I felt mortified, on the other, protective. I knew that his shaking was a sign of his belief in the awesomeness of the task he conducted. He literally trembled before what he believed to be the presence of God.

I was astounded at those moments by his vulnerability and depth of his faith and afraid of the enormous gap I saw growing between us. How could we respect each other, know each other, when I saw him as a victim of blind devotion, and imagined, in turn, that he saw me as a failure at life's greatest mission — to love and serve God.

My father died of a heart attack when I was twenty-one. Shortly before his death, he developed a nervous habit of praying obsessively. His lips moved constantly, his head bowing up and down at the dinner table, in the car, while watching TV.

I've only learned recently how ill he was at that time. I wish I would have known then, the seriousness of his condition.

Some memories still haunt me. I see him in a corner, alone, praying. At the time, I thought he was just being neurotic, now I know he was afraid. I wish I could go back and put my arms around him. We wouldn't have to talk about God. I could just tell him that I love him.

*

Sins of the Fathers

A year and a half after my father's death, I was married in Heinz Chapel, a non-denominational chapel on the campus of the University of Pittsburgh. I had asked the head priest of our hometown parish — Father Walter Benz — to officiate at the ceremony. He and my father had been close. A tall, imposing silver-haired man of my father's generation, Father Benz looked more like George C. Scott playing a corporate CEO than any priest we had seen in our small town. He drove new, expensive model cars. I want to say Cadillac or Lincoln Town Car, but perhaps it was only a large Buick. The rumor mill declared him an only child from a rich family. Either because of his last name or the fancy cars he drove, we imagined him the heir to the Mercedes-Benz fortune. To us, he seemed an elegant, sophisticated presence amidst a largely undereducated population heavy on second- and third-generation Italians, Poles, Irish, and Czechs.

Father Benz presided over my father's funeral and gave a moving eulogy. But he declined to officiate at my wedding. He said he didn't approve of non-denominational places of worship. Vatican rules don't prohibit priests from performing services at chapels, but Father Benz said he preferred to administer sacraments in an official Catholic church.

I was disappointed but accepted his decision. He was a man of principle, I told myself, and he couldn't compromise.

Seventeen years later, in September 1998, front-page newspaper stories in the Pittsburgh *Post Gazette* zapped the man-of-principle theory forever. The article reported that Father Walter Benz "was accused" and "allegedly admitted stealing $1,000 a week for 20 years" at two suburban churches, one of which was our hometown church, Blessed Sacrament. According to subsequent articles, he used the money "for gambling trips with a church secretary."

Because he was terminally ill, the police decided against arraignment.

On a theological level, the failures of Father Benz crystallized concerns that had been growing inside me for years—that those who interpret religion are capable of making mistakes, not only in their own lives, but also in matters of guidance; and that those who interpret religion have been limited, until very recently, to those who are male.

Who are these men? These priests? As a child, I had wondered about the nuns, those who were merely servants of the Church, women who could mess up a child's school day if they were in a bad mood, but who were powerless when it came to eternity. As an adult, I began to question the priests—those considered the emissaries of God on earth, the gatekeepers to the kingdom.

In the years I went to church, 1959 to 1980, I heard many priests rail against birth control and abortion, yet never once in my estimated 1,100 attendances at mass (we went on Fridays in Catholic school as well as Sundays) did I hear a priest condemn or even mention rape or sexual abuse, crimes that, as an adult, I read about almost daily in newspapers. I heard many a sermon about the role of women in the home, but I never once heard a priest mention domestic violence.

These became major issues for me as I opened my eyes to the realities of the world. I was infuriated at memories of priests badgering women to be better, more modest, more obedient. When priests raged against abortion, they never addressed the events— sometimes criminal—that led to an unwanted pregnancy. Why didn't they ever scold the men? Is the submission and control of women some complicated, religious prescription for peace on earth? If so, it's not working.

As far as I'm concerned, legions of books could be written—and probably are—on this subject. Suffice it to say that in the eighties and nineties, my feminist anger spread beyond the Catholic Church to other religions that degrade and negate women: religions, or sects of religions, that today don't allow women to initiate a divorce, speak in church, seek custody of children, get an education, file charges against an abusive husband, or even hang on to their genitalia, to name a few.

The more I looked, the more examples of female exclusion and marginalization, big and small, I found.

For instance, my sister attended pre-Cana (wedding preparation) classes in the early eighties. She and her fiancé sat down at school desks with the rest of the class. A man, part of the lay couple teaching the course, stood up and wrote in large capital letters on the blackboard: KISS THE PENIS. After the laughter died down, the couple went on to promote this as an alternative to intercourse when the stars weren't right for natural birth control. "Remember ladies, kiss the penis," was the rallying cry for the day. Not only did he give my brother-in-law a one-liner to employ for the rest of his life, but the instructor also failed to mention the reciprocal act.

For me, that line, Kiss the Penis, underscored perfectly the conscious and unconscious male-worshipping aspects of male-centered religions. It could almost be a chant or a hymn. I can see a priest at the altar raising the chalice. "Kiss the Penis," he would say, as an altar boy rings the bells.

Despite my anger, after my father died in 1981, I actually considered returning to the Church he loved. Death and loss do this to people, make them start looking around for hope, for answers to the big meaning-of-life questions. And I was not immune to that calling. I turned toward the only spiritual home I knew. "Inactive Catholics Rediscover Your Faith," read the banners flying from many a church.

I decided to start at the beginning. I bought a Bible. I thought if I'm going to rediscover Christianity, I better read the instructions. However, despite my best intentions, I didn't get far. Lot stopped me cold.

"Before they had gone to bed, all the men from every part of the city of Sodom—both young and old—surrounded the house. They called to Lot, "Where are the men who came to you tonight? Bring them out to us so that we can have sex with them." Lot went outside to meet them and shut the door behind him and said, "No, my friends. Don't do this wicked thing. Look, I have two daughters who have never slept with a man. Let me bring them out to you, and you can do what you like with them. But don't do anything to these men, for they have come under the protection of my roof."Genesis 19: 4-8

What's going on here? Lot, the moral center in this story, is offering up his daughters to be gang raped? When I investigated further, I found that this is one of the passages most likely to be used against gays and lesbians. The general evangelical Christian interpretation is that the "sin" of homosexuality is deemed greater than that of raping girls or giving up one's daughters to be raped.

I was shocked by the evilness of this story. The more I read about the God of the Old Testament, the more I saw a portrait of a power who inspired demented worship and endless slaughter in his name, a God who seemed more like a petty dictator and arrogant egomaniac than the all-knowing, all-loving God of my youth.

*

Desperately Seeking Something

After all this ranting, it may be hard to understand that I had both my children baptized. Neither my husband nor I believed at that point, but two things made me do it: family politics and fear. Eight years in Catholic School had left its mark, visions of limbo, purgatory, and hell danced in my head. Just in case I was wrong, I wanted my children to have that insurance policy.

As my children grew, I faced another dilemma. Despite my ambiguity, I felt obligated to give them some type of religious education. At least they'd have something to reject when they became teenagers.

So I called upon the Methodists, Episcopalians (whom I'm told are similar to Catholics without the Pope), Quakers, and Buddhists. I ended up with the Unitarian Universalists. This self-described "church of the open mind" does not adhere to a particular dogma, which means that technically it's not a religion, more of an ethical society.

I bought my children a book, *What Is God?* It says things like, "Maybe God is what you feel when you stand on a very high mountain." "If everything is God, Then I am God, You are God, All of us are God!"

This concept was as new to me as it was to my daughters, since I basically had been led to believe that God was an old man, a pretty mean one at that, who sat on a throne, picked on his son, and sometimes transmuted into an entity called the Holy Spirit, or, in old-fashioned terms, the Holy Ghost.

I found another book, *Heart Talks with Mother God.* According to this, the Bible uses "feminine images" to describe God's love. The authors present the following interpretation: "God is like a nurturing mother feeding her suckling infant at her breast (Isa 49:15; 66:11-13)."

God as both man and woman? Why had I never heard this mentioned before? Heretofore, I thought modern man had created God in his image alone, a bit of megalomania unrivaled in the universe. If only God could be represented as both mother and father, I could get into this.

But alas, God is not. Maybe some day.

In 1992, the Church of England voted to allow the ordination of women as priests. The Episcopalians followed suit in 1997. Also that year, the Catholic Theological Society of America unanimously resolved that the Vatican was not infallible in its ruling excluding women as priests and called for further study of the subject. Due to a shortage of priests and growing pressure from progressive segments in the church, many believe that in several generations women will be ordained as Catholic priests.

But by that point, I'll be dead. So to my list of vices—doubter, rebel, traitor—I add another: impatient.

*

The Mystery

My mother kept for many years a Catholic Elementary School primer, which I loved. It had a passage that said, to the best of my recollection: "What is electricity? No one knows. God made electricity. God is a mystery."

If asked today to give a quick scientific summary of electricity, I couldn't. So I can see the appeal of returning to the mystery: I don't know. God made electricity.

It's hard being out there without a dogma to hang onto.

I still have pinned in my purse a St. Christopher's medal; it says, "I am a Catholic, in case of accident notify a priest." In my bedroom I keep my father's worn wooden rosary beads, the lacy Spanish silver rosary beads I received for my Confirmation, and a two-inch silver-plate cross pendant with a small crystal circle in the center, which contains The Lord's Prayer in the tiniest print imaginable.

I treasure these objects. They comfort me. But I can't fool myself. They aren't holy relics anymore, but the souvenirs of more innocent days.

I no longer have the faith of my father. But does that mean I no longer have faith?

The magical, mystical sense of the sublime I used to get from light streaming in through the stained-glass windows of a cathedral, I now get from light streaming in through the bare branches of trees in the woods.

When I look at my daughters—as babies sleeping in my arms, as children rolling in the leaves, as teenagers dressing for the dance—I get a glimpse into that abstract slogan, God is love.

When I see an ambulance parked outside the school—lights flashing, paramedics running with a stretcher—and I know my daughter is one of a handful of students inside practicing gymnastic stunts, I am instantly snared in that age-old web of fear and God. Who wouldn't I strike a bargain with at such a moment?

For some, for me, the oceans of doubt and faith will forever churn together.

But that's all right.

I have always loved islands. I love to stand on the edge of the water and imagine myself adrift in a big, blue sea. At those moments, I don't feel that nihilistic, existential terror of "I am but a speck in the universe" and "food for the worms." I feel an excitement, an all-encompassing almost electrical connection. And I am open to that electricity, to that mystery, which I am told is God.

φ

SACRAMENT
Julia Park Tracey

IN THE MIDDLE OF THE NIGHT he rises with a groan, and goes to the bathroom. I can never hear him pee because he sits down, as though too exhausted to remain standing. He's the only man I've ever known who pees that way.

The toilet flushes, and he comes back to the bedroom, pulls on pants and shirt, leans over to kiss me goodbye. "See you at Mass," he says, and is gone.

As soon as the front door shuts, I roll to his side of the bed, still warm, his pillow still indented, his scent in the sheets. I lie in his place until I hear the sound of his car's motor growl to life and the muffler's rattle. I hear him back out of the driveway; even in the silence of the suburban night, the sound of the engine quickly fades. I breathe his scent. I drift to sleep.

In the morning, I shower and dress for Mass in a plaid skirt and a sweater, black loafers—Catholic schoolgirl chic. I drink my coffee quickly, knowing that I've broken the rule, that I should have fasted an hour before receiving Holy Communion. But it's death without coffee—a headache like a hangover—and I must wake up, so I drink it anyway and drive to church. *Forgive me, Father.*

I always sit in the same place at Mass, center section, near the left hand aisle. The priest always enters up the left aisle and exits down the right. When he distributes Communion, he stands at the left, while the deacon stands at the right. If I sat at the right, our eyes would meet as he departed, and he might reach out a hand to touch mine as he passed, as he does with other parishioners. But on the left, he and I are intimate in the giving and receiving of Communion. I genuflect deeply—my knee rests at the nubby carpet for a full five seconds as I bless myself *In the name of the Father, and the Son, and the Holy Spirit*— then slide into my pew and pull down the kneeler.

The choir tunes up and I close my eyes. The rich notes fill my ears and the cantor invites us to sing. I haven't prayed yet, so I whisper, "Thank You, God, for this blessed day," and stand to sing. I know the words to the hymn—we sing it almost every week—and find its page easily in the missal. I sing clearly but not too loudly as the procession begins. The altar boys enter first, one carrying the tall processional cross, the other swinging the thurible of incense. The lector follows with the big red book, the Lectionary, held above her head. A second lector follows her, then the deacon.

The priest brushes past in the aisle like a prince, his chasuble gilded with embroidered wheat stalks and clusters of grapes, symbols of the Eucharist, of fertility, of spiritual food and drink.

He crosses behind the altar, bows and kisses it. Then he returns to the front and sings with the rest of us to the end of the song. I can see his face, between the heads in the pews in front of me. It's as if he puts on a persona when he pulls the chasuble over his head: Priest, Holy Man, The Good Father. He's got to be an icon for the people, God's representative on earth. When we lie in bed, he tells me funny stories about the other priests in the diocese, about something the Bishop said yesterday, comic slices of parish life. But there in his chair at the front of the church, he seems to glow with a holy aura. I think I can see a white luminescence around him, or is it a trick of the light?

His voice is deep and rich. When he gives the homily, I know he is speaking to me. His voice carries a certain inflection; it flickers and parries and drives into me like a tongue of fire. I think of the timbre of his words and how he speaks to me in bed, in the dark, the same low rumble that he uses in the confessional, soft enough so others won't hear. The bass vibration moves inside me, as if it reaches some receptor at its lowest pitch, purrs me into life, into delight. He asks us to stand and pray, and I think of him straining over me, of the sound he makes when he comes.

We sing again, we sit, we stand, we kneel. He passes to the altar, stands behind it with his arms upraised. The altar before him is wide and low like a bed, covered with a white cloth; we pull it back and slip into its coolness together. I know the shape of his birthmark. I know the color of his toothbrush. I know the smell of his skin.

We rise, we kneel again. *Father, I am not worthy to receive you, only say the word and I shall be healed.* Only say the word and I shall be yours.

The rows begin to shuffle forward for Communion. I slide toward the left aisle and wait my turn. Soon enough, the line moves forward, and I cup my hands together, left inside the right. I hold his balls gently in my hand when I take him in my mouth, my hand cupped just so. I reach the front of the line. He is there.

"The Body of Christ," he says, and presses the thin slice into my hand — not the small round wafer that the others receive, but a piece of the priest's own larger wafer, blessed and broken and shared with me.

"Amen," I say, and place it on my tongue. I bless myself and pass to the right.

The deacon passes me the chalice. "The Blood of Christ."

"Amen," I say again, and sip the warm red wine like honeyed blood. I follow the line back up the aisle, back to my seat, back to my knees. "Let me always remember the sweetness of this day," I pray.

Too soon the Mass is ended. "Go in peace to love and serve the Lord," he says from the front.

"Thanks be to God," we reply in unison, and again the shuffle begins, out toward the back as the chorus sings us away and the priest and the deacon and all their train sweep past.

He stands outside the doors, his hand outstretched to the stream of parishioners. Everyone wants to shake his hand. Everyone wants to talk to him. The ladies kiss him. The men all have a joke to tell. He throws his head back and laughs like a tolling of bells. Everyone else laughs, too. I wait my turn, slowly as the line moves; I could shoulder past and see him later, but I can't. I have to do this — shake his hand, feel the pressure of his fingers, see the smile in his eyes.

And there it is — the pressure, the look, the electric slide of skin on skin. We smile. We part. No one sees or knows.

At home, I eat breakfast, clean the bathroom and vacuum the apartment. I read the paper. I do a little laundry. I paint my nails, two coats of Rose Petal. I run to the store for a bottle of wine. I check my messages when I return but there are none. Later, when the sun finally sets, I throw a frozen dinner in the microwave and eat it with a book propped open. I clean the kitchen, careful of my nails. I bathe in bubbles scented with lavender, clean and fresh. I shave my legs. I put on a dressing gown, the one with the little blue flowers, and wait.

φ

BANTE

Ellen Bryson

YOU ARE FORTY-FOUR YEARS OLD and were once a therapist from Houston. You have one sister. She is younger than you are and has been lost to someone else's fundamentalism. That's it. That's all the background you ever gave me. When you were ordained they renamed you U Suruttama: an unwieldy, heavy name compared to that silvery body of yours. You accepted the difficulty of your name then allowed the rest of us to call you Bante. *Bante*, the Sanskrit word for monk. Monk. Mr. Monk. I picture you sitting beneath the pine trees, shaded by tradition, renunciation, a generic name. Your sandaled feet are lightly crossed, one long white foot swaying against your saffron robe. If you let your hair grow back, would it be the same color as that robe, I wonder. Or maybe you've just shaved an already balding head. But vanity belongs to the layman, doesn't it, Bante? Not to you.

Do you remember teaching me about the duck? This was days before the lightening. We sat in the main house study, door discreetly open.(What precept is it that doesn't allow you to be in a closed room with a woman?) I said: "My mother. Jesus, I hate my mother. I really have tried to forgive her, but how can I? All those men, all that humiliation, and the worst part is ..."

"NOW!" you yelled, interrupting me mid-sentence.

I jumped.

You grinned and your nostrils flailed. "Feel your jaw!"

"Pardon me?"

"You're lost in your own story and it shows in your jaw."

I was angry then. "You're not being very sensitive."

"Just feel it," you said. "Just try."

I tried.

"It's heavy, isn't it?"

I nodded.

"So quack."

Christ, I thought. This I do not need.

"Like the duck from those old Groucho Marx's shows."

"The duck."

"Yeah. Remember when someone said something right? How the duck would fall out of nowhere. Make a stupid noise. Be the duck."

I hid a smile.

"DO IT!" you demanded and, surprised, I croaked out, "Quack." A pause. And I laughed out loud.

"Your past is just a story," you said proudly. "Nothing to do about it. Just be aware of it, then laugh like hell at yourself."

I thought about my mother then. What exactly had she done? This always takes me a second. She behaved in a most unseemly fashion, that much is true. And, at least according to my father, a mother with lovers, and many of them, is too primitive a beast to allow into the inner realms of heaven's cleaner rooms, but she did give me gifts.

She gave the gift of passion and of primitive joy.

And the gift of a woman not afraid of being herself.

Later you gave me a wink to remind me. You whispered in my ear, "Let the sky open," and I envisioned my mother, primitive and angry, throwing thunderbolts from the sky. She was dressed like a duck and once again, I laughed.

*

On the Day of Lightening, it was nearly ninety. Have you noticed, Bante, we both have the same kind of skin? Soft, thin, yellow overtones. And prone to sweat. We sat together in separate chairs, talking quietly about facts and about things that go against facts, about this world and the alien one sitting right next to it, a breath away. It was so hot that afternoon I had to pull the hair away from the back of my neck. Our bodies barely moved. We talked and talked, tossing up facts high above our sweltering heads. Up went my mother, AND her body, my father following quickly after. Then less concrete images, like forgiveness, understanding, and the newly understood concept of life beyond story, of life beyond life. We moved on. "This is how to smell a truth." "Here's how to remember who you are in the dark." Each fact seemed to rise on its own, not caring who it came from, no preference for context, age, or gender. We alternated as the sky outside darkened. Weightless and evanescent, thoughts sparkled and snapped, and when two thoughts intertwined, they emitted such a frenzy of color that it embarrassed both of us. Even though we changed our aim, more and more of our thoughts started to cross, sparking and dancing together until the sky filled with thunder.

Eventually the rains came. But not until much, much later.

The Persians have a creation myth about the world's first set of parents. These joyous, loving people were given the gift of bearing two children at once, but on first seeing their offspring, the first parents were so overwhelmed that, out of love, they ate them.

God, in his infinite wisdom, reduced their capacity to love some 99%.

Does that sound cynical? Because somewhere I recognize a greater love, I really do. (Even my cat can evoke it in me.) Did you know, Bante, that the word "cynic" is from the Greek "kynikos," meaning literally "like a dog?" I picture the mutt: old flea bitten Greek dog, ribs out to here, tail slipped between bony flanks as it pulls its red lips back to reveal yellow canines and blackened gums. This dog grins and dances an ingratiating little shuffle in hope of food. His love is all about hunger and mine is not like that, at least not always. It's a passion for a long forgotten ideal.

So perhaps I have to be more honest about that afternoon. About how, underneath it lay the demon of the body, sweating alongside the two of us. Red-faced and heavy-jawed, I can still hear the snap of its saliva-covered teeth clicking together in anticipation. It's breath (could I actually SEE it, cutting icy waves across the steaming room) smelled of wet clay and earthworms. Do you remember those little oval tubes of colored paper that the Chinese make? Slip one on your fingers and be caught forever. Once on, never off, and struggle makes it inevitable. If I don't finish with the truth now, I might be lost forever in some perverse kind of daydream, some psychological finger twister.

I wanted you.

And I think you wanted me.

*

The rains came the day the forest monks made their visits. They spoke only Thai and looked like pleasant little animals scratching themselves and laughing in an unholy fashion. You ran their visit like a Day Care, making sure they washed for lunch and that the rice wasn't over-boiled. Sometime after lunch I caught your eye. Standing on the upstairs landing, I looked down as you passed. I smiled and motioned you to join me, but you pretended to misread my signal and kept on walking.

At first I thought it was the presence of the forest monks. The confusion of foreign elements. But you stayed at that distance for the rest of that day, and the next, and the next after that. I started to wait in places I knew you would pass. Once I caught myself walking with an exaggerated swing of hip, like the dog and his grin and his hungry little dance.

Okay.

I understood then.

Perhaps the mistakes of one's parents are destined to be repeated. Maybe our walls crack open now and again, allowing us to slip through and out. Maybe not. But it seems a useful way to use one's story. I think one can use it to duck out when the going gets a little too familiar.

And so, with a not-so-pleasant smile and a quack, I left you there.

φ

MIRACLE
Jyotsna Sreenivasan

I DON'T KNOW WHETHER I SHOULD BE WORRIED about my wife or not. I
still don't understand exactly why she did it, although we've talked
about it a lot. Her hair was attractive, but she's beautiful to me even
now. What I'm concerned about is the reason behind doing it. Or the
lack of reason. People who are very exceptional—geniuses, or saints—
do odd things. But so do people who are mad or unbalanced in some
way. I haven't seen signs of anything strange about her yet, but neither
have I seen signs of exceptionality. Of course I love Meera, and I
wouldn't leave her even if she were mad. I wouldn't accuse her
parents of trying to pass her off as normal when they showed her to
me at the bride-viewing. I'm not that kind of man, although I know
some Indian men who are like that.

One reason I wanted to marry her is that she seemed so
unexceptional—so content, quiet, and happy with herself. She was not
flashy or striving after anything, whether it was material wealth or
status or some kind of uniqueness. Now she tells me that when we
met, she was full of longing for something, she didn't even know
what.

Meera and I met one year ago, in India. I had been in the U.S. for
quite a few years and my parents had been bothering me about
marriage for some time. They wanted me to come back home and
choose a bride. For a long time I put them off with excuses—I was
finishing my thesis, and then I was looking for a job, and then I had a
new job and was trying to get my citizenship. Actually, I had the idea
that I should find my own wife. I was a modern young man. Why
should I go to India and let my parents hunt up some girl for me?

But for whatever reason, I did not find the girl I was looking for in
the U.S. I went to a lot of Indian events on campus and around town—
Diwali festivals and Hindustani music concerts and screenings of old
Hindi movies—and some of the girls were pretty, and some were
friendly, and some were both. I liked a few girls but by the time I
figured out how dating worked, and then figured out which girls
might be okay with the concept of dating, and then by the time I got
up the courage to actually ask a girl to go out, that girl had either

moved away or had taken up with some other boy. So finally I thought I'd better go home and let my parents fix me up. There was no point pretending to be some kind of Romeo.

Meera grew up in a small town in Karnataka, the same state I'm from, but I grew up in our state's largest city, Bangalore. I'd never been to her town before I met her and when my parents and I arrived, it was at the end of the rainy season and the place seemed like paradise, after the noise and dust of Bangalore. Every green plant that could grow was growing. The palm trees along the roads were dripping with leaves. The bougainvillea bushes were bursting with red blooms. The air was scented with jasmine. And it was so quiet. I think the loudest noise I heard was the clanging of the goat bells, when the goat woman walked by every morning and every evening shooing her animals along the road.

I think I fell in love with the town as well as with Meera, but now Meera says that the town was awful—she was so bored. No one did anything but gossip and watch old movies on TV and do one *pooja* after another.

I don't remember much about Meera's parents' house because I was only there to see Meera. My parents and I were sitting on the sofa and she came in and did *namaskar* to us all. She was wearing a pale pink sari and she looked really sweet. Her skin is fair, and I'm not one of those people who think that dark-skinned women are ugly, but the pink sari really did make her face glow in a soft way. She's a small girl, thin and graceful. I liked her right away.

We didn't talk then—that was in the afternoon—but that evening I took her out for dinner. We didn't say anything particularly significant, but one thing I remember is that she said she'd never really talked to a boy before, except for her brother and her cousins. I believed it. Especially in a small town, girls are so sheltered in India.

She seemed very calm during our dinner, but now she tells me that she was wild with excitement. She kept thinking of how it would be if she were to touch me! I'm sure I would have loved that—I was wild to touch her too. Even though I'd chatted with a lot of girls, I had never even held a girl's hand, if you can believe it.

So I took her back to her house, and told my parents I agreed to marry her, and she told her parents she agreed to marry me. We performed the wedding about a week later, went on a honeymoon to Kerala, and then I took her to my parents' house in Bangalore. After that, I had to come back here because my vacation had ended. Since I was already a U.S. citizen I got Meera a visa fairly quickly, and she was able to join me a few months later. It wasn't a long separation compared to how long some couples must be apart, but for me it was horrible. I missed her so much. I couldn't stand sleeping by myself after having slept with her for ten nights straight. Meera says it wasn't so bad for her because it was all very exciting—shopping and seeing sights in Bangalore when she stayed with my parents—so much better than the dull town she grew up in. She felt that being married and coming to the U.S. was what she had been waiting for.

At first, she says, life in the U.S. was very exciting. We bought a new house—had it built for us in a new development outside of Washington, DC, so there was all that to do—selecting the options we wanted, the wallpaper, the carpeting, and so on. She found a job. Her field is computer programming. We went on trips to see the cherry blossoms and monuments in D.C., all the sights in New York City, the Luray Caverns and Shenandoah forest.

Looking back, Meera did tell me one significant thing. One night, several months ago, we were lying in bed just before going to sleep, and Meera started whispering something to me. There were only the two of us in the house so I didn't know why she was whispering.

"I want to tell you something that happened when I was fifteen," she said.

I was feeling sleepy, and I yawned. Meera shook me and said, "Listen! Listen to me." So I blinked and stretched and tried to stay awake.

"When I was fifteen we went to Tirupati, just as we did every year," she said. "We climbed the hill. We stood in line to see the idol. And when we were in front of the idol, I thought it was God himself looking at me."

I didn't know why she was telling me this story. I have been to Tirupati many times, of course. It is one of the most famous pilgrimage sites in South India, and my family visited very often. The subject was not at all interesting to me. At that time I was having a flare-up of a rash I sometimes get, so I was bothered by itching on the inside of my elbow.

"I thought it was Sri Venkateshwara himself looking at me," she repeated.

"Maybe it was," I said. I rubbed my elbow, trying not to scratch. "You know the idol is supposed to have been created by Sri Venkateshwara himself. It is not supposed to have been carved by human hands."

"I don't believe any of that," she said.

"Then why are you telling me this story?"

"I want you to know what happened. I went there. At that time I believed in God just like anyone else did. And I saw God looking at me. I started weeping. And out loud I said that I would shave my head."

"Everyone shaves their heads at Tirupati."

"Not in our families. You know that women do not shave their heads in our families. The women promise to undertake a fast or something, but it is only the men and children who get their heads shaved."

"Yes, that's true. Why did you promise that, then?"

"It just came over me. I don't know. I can't explain it. And then Amma was so angry. She thought I would look low-class with a shaved head. But we had to go through with it. Everyone heard my promise. Amma thought it would be very bad luck not to get it done. She took me right then to one of the barbers."

My elbow was really itching by this time. I got up and went into the bathroom to put some hydrocortisone cream on it. When I came back to bed, Meera was sitting up.

"Listen," she said. She was now speaking loudly.

I crawled into bed and lay down but didn't close my eyes.

"After I got my head shaved," she said, "my friends at school really gave me a hard time. One of my friends said, don't you know that statue is nothing but a rock? This girl said she was an atheist. I was so ignorant; I thought it was some kind of new religion! I had to look it up in the dictionary. Then when I found out what it meant—I knew. I knew there was no God. I knew I had been deceived."

"Then why did you think you saw God looking at you?" I asked.

"It was nothing," she said. "You know how it is, standing in that line for hours. You get hot and tired. And as you get closer to the idol, the incense is so thick you can hardly breathe. And once you are in front of the idol, there are so many *deepas* flickering there, and the idol is black, you can't really see the face at all. It was just a trick my brain played on me."

"You never know," I said. "Maybe it really was a miracle. Maybe God really did look at you."

"How can you say such a thing? You are a scientist."

"Some scientists are atheists. But for me, studying physics and astronomy has made me realize how much there is about the universe that we don't know."

"That is no proof of God," she said. "Just because we don't know everything yet, that doesn't prove God exists."

I didn't say anything. I was surprised to learn that she was an atheist, but it was okay with me. To each his own and all of that.

Then she turned on the light. "Do you believe in miracles?" she demanded.

"Yes," I said. I closed my eyes to shut out the glare of the light. "I've never experienced a miracle, but I think there is a possibility that miracles can happen."

"That's ridiculous," she said. "How can you say that? You are so educated."

I didn't know why she was so agitated, especially since she was the one who brought the whole thing up, and she was the one who claimed to be an atheist. I thought maybe she'd had a stressful day at work or something.

After that conversation, things seemed to go back to normal, but now Meera says that she started thinking about miracles and God all the time. I had no idea. She says she started noticing articles in the newspaper about miracles. She was surprised at first that people in America cared about miracles. She thought that was just an old-fashioned Indian thing. There was one article about an eggplant. It seems when this eggplant was cut open, the seeds formed a pattern that spelled "Allah" in Arabic. She says there was a photo in the paper, but I don't remember it. I do remember that we ate a lot of eggplant dishes at that time. She says, when she cut open the eggplants, she never saw any pattern in a language she could read.

But now we come to the miracle that she claims she did see. A few days ago, on her way to work, Meera was stopped at a traffic light and she saw a little homemade sign by the road that said, this way to the Virgin Mary miracle or some such thing. So she turned and went that way. She never even went to work. She followed those homemade signs to a small shopping center. When she got out of the car she thought, I've made a mistake, because the people she saw were of the low-class type. So, she thought, I don't belong here. It's not that she's biased — I'm not biased either — but we come from very educated, well-off families. But she stayed because she thought she might as well see this thing that they were calling a miracle.

There was quite a long line. She asked what the miracle was, and someone told her that a picture of the Virgin Mary had appeared, all by itself, on the side of a building. She waited and waited. She was the only one there in office clothes. A lot of people were holding beads and praying. Some people tried to kneel, but the police made them stand again. That's how many people there were — they needed police to control the crowd. It was hot and there was no shade. Meera took off her suit jacket but still she felt warm. Finally she reached the front of the line, and all she saw was a blank wall. The paint was peeling and sort of patchy. There was a black woman standing next to her, and Meera whispered that she didn't see anything, and that woman said, just keep looking. Don't even blink. Then Meera realized it was some kind of optical illusion. These people were so primed to see the Virgin Mary that their brains somehow created an image out of the pattern of paint on the wall. She was about to turn around and leave. She would still have been on time for work.

But just as she was about to turn, she saw it. She said it popped right out at her. It looked like a real face of a woman, not a painting. It was three-dimensional. It even moved a little. The face looked so kind, so compassionate, Meera said. She couldn't take her eyes off it. She felt the face was trying to tell her something, and she kept trying to listen, to comprehend, but there were a lot of people behind her, pushing her aside to see the image, and she had to get out of line.

As she stepped aside, the black woman next to her stepped out of line also, and Meera said they looked at each other and threw their arms around each other. This is very unlike Meera. In our families, we do not give hugs all the time like people in America do. I'm not saying it's right or wrong to give hugs to strangers, it's just not what we do.

But Meera said she did it without even thinking. She hugged this fat black woman in the parking lot of that shopping center.

Then the black woman went away and Meera stood there. She said she felt so happy. She didn't want to go on to work. She thought about getting back in line to see the Virgin Mary again, but instead she turned and saw a barbershop behind her. She went into this barbershop and asked the barber to shave her head. And he did it. I suppose he'd do anything as long as he got paid. He didn't care if the person was unbalanced or not. She came straight home after that, and when I got home from work that's when I saw her and found out what she'd done.

As soon as I entered the house, I knew something was up because there was no food cooked. Meera is usually very prompt with dinner. She plans the meals over the weekend, and she even chops vegetables the night before or in the morning, before she goes to work. If she's making *dosa*, she puts the *dal* and rice to soak the day before. So as I said, as soon as I came home I noticed there was no food on the stove.

I called her name, and she called back from upstairs. I went upstairs. In here, she called. She was in our bedroom. And then I saw.

She was sitting on the floor, with a suitcase open in front of her and a big smile on her face.

"What do you think?" she asked. She seemed excited and a little nervous at the same time.

I was in shock, as you can imagine. I sat on the bed and she told me the whole story. She even asked me to feel her head.

"It's so soft and smooth," she said. "I don't remember this from the last time. My mother was so upset and my friends made fun of me. I became ashamed. I began to regret my promise as soon as I made it. I wanted to do it right this time. My hair is a gift to God. This time I will not regret it."

"Couldn't it have been the same as last time?" I asked. "At Tirupati, you were hot and tired, and you thought God was looking at you. Now, you were hot and tired, and again you see a religious image looking at you. Maybe it was just a trick your brain played on you."

"No, that's not it," Meera said. "Even in Tirupati, it was really God looking at me. That moment was the happiest of my life. I felt blissful."

"Then why did you become an atheist?" I asked. "If you felt so blissful, why did you stop believing?"

She shrugged, but she was still smiling. "I was a teenager," she said. "At that time it really mattered what other people thought. And then, when I realized there were people who didn't believe in God, I thought, maybe I'm the one who is duped. Maybe that's why everyone is making fun of me."

I don't completely understand Meera's explanation. Why should it matter so much whether other people believe or not? But that's what she said.

"Ever since that time," she said, "I've been looking for that same feeling. And now I've found it."

In the suitcase in front of her were a lot of *pooja* articles — pictures of gods and goddesses, silver idols and *kumkum* boxes, incense holders, that sort of thing. Her mother had packed them for Meera, but Meera had never set them up. She asked if I would mind if she used the den downstairs for her *pooja* room. I said that was fine with me — we didn't use the den anyway. We have three bedrooms upstairs, and on the main floor the living room, dining room, and kitchen. The den and family room are in the walkout basement. We hardly use most of this space.

Then she looked up at me with her big eyes and said, "I'm going to quit my job."

I said, "If you don't want to work, that's okay. My salary is more than enough for both of us. As far as I'm concerned, your job was just something to keep you from being bored at home all day."

"It's not that I don't want to work," she said. "It's that I don't know what work I am meant to do. I don't know what God wants me to do."

That's when my shock started to turn into worry. Was she going to become some kind of Mother Teresa? Was she going to insist upon serving the poor? Not that I have anything against that, but you have to know what you are getting into. It's not child's play. Most of us are not cut out for that kind of thing.

But I didn't say any of this to her. I just said, "Fine. You do whatever you want. It's fine with me." I thought maybe the whole thing would blow over soon.

She called her office right away and left a message with her boss that she was quitting. No two-week notice. I mentioned to her that this would not be good if she wanted to get recommendations for future jobs, but she insisted that she had to quit right away.

Besides this impulsiveness, she doesn't seem mad, in particular. She cooks the meals just as she used to. She takes care of her clothing and appearance and that sort of thing. I did notice that she has taken off some of her jewelry. She's still wearing her wedding necklace and the wedding ring we bought together once she came to the U.S, but she no longer wears her diamond earrings or gold bangles.

She has spent the past few days converting the den into a *pooja* room. She set up a low coffee table as an altar, on which she arranged her silver idols. Behind this she hung a large batik of Lakshmi sitting on a lotus. She propped up other framed pictures of deities—Ganesha, Rama and Sita, and so forth—on the floor around the table, and hung silk-flower garlands on them. These are the usual things that Hindu women do. As long as she doesn't spend all her time praying, I have no problem with it.

Right now she's in her shrine. That's what I call it. I peek in and see her sitting on the floor facing her altar. I want to go in and tap her on the shoulder and say, come on, let's drive to the mall. But I just stand here in the doorway. She's like one of those Tibetan boy monks, with her shaved head and her orange *salvar kameez*. She looks so different that I feel like I've never really known her. The smoke swirls up from the incense stick and hangs in the air around her. The scent is strong in that stuffy room, and I turn away to get a breath of fresh air.

When I look back, I don't see Meera. I see only Lakshmi, larger than life, smiling down at me and holding up a hand in blessing. Then I notice my wife standing at the side of the room. She picks up a banana from the altar and holds it out to me. Her eyes are wet with tears.

"Come here," she says. She's smiling sweetly, and I can recognize something of my Meera again.

I've been taught that it's bad luck to refuse *prasada*—food blessed by God. So I step into the dim room and walk through the incense smoke, toward the Lakshmi with the hand raised in blessing. Meera rests her fuzzy head against my shoulder for a moment. I take the banana, peel and eat it, with Meera and the gods looking on.

φ

BEATNIK
Fred A. Wilcox

Misfits

FROG WOMAN IS HAVING A BAD DAY. It's been snowing all morning, wind howling through the trees. Radiators sputter and hiss. I move my destroyer across the board. Bobby Lee counterattacks. We watch him closely because he cheats. A pretty young woman winks at me. Last week, doctors closed deep gashes in her forearms. Frog Woman releases a Baritone hiccup. She moves her battleship across the board, sinks Bobby's ship and tries, without success, to stop croaking. It is still dark when deputies escort Frog Woman into the parking lot. On these mornings, a deep empathic silence spreads through the ward. Eggs congeal on breakfast plates; coffee turns tepid, then cold. We watch them huff and puff, fat gun-toting bears. Our friend will go quietly. She knows, we know, that she's not crazy. One night, a spotted green reptile crawled inside of her. She can't seem to convince this creature to leave. Most of the time he's comatose, but now and again he gets rowdy.

The bears will drive her to Marion State Hospital where, we've heard, a mad doctor roams the wards, cutting patterns into inmates — we refuse to call ourselves "patients" — skulls. On the back wards, people are shackled naked to walls. Somewhere between the hog farm and the cow barn, bodies are dumped into icy pits, leaving no evidence that they ever walked the earth.

Once they take you off to the snake pit, no one will ever hear from you again.

*

Most of the inmates in Fairlawns are women. At night, the warning siren goes off. Lights flash. Doors open and close. Bodies are strapped to gurneys. When they recover enough to be allowed onto open ward, I ask them why they tried to kill themselves. One woman confides that her husband—she calls him "pig man"—spends his days scavenging mountains of burning rat-filled garbage.

"No sooner walks in the door than he wants sex," says Marlene. "'Now listen here,' I tell him. 'You stink like a damn old pig. Now get in there and put some water on your dirty old self, Luther. Might think about it then.'

"Luther blows his stack. 'You're my wife,' he says, 'and you'll do as you're told.'"

Marlene calls her husband's mother. Maybe she'll talk some sense into this man's dumb head. She tells Mrs. Wilkie that Luther hasn't bathed in weeks. Looks like a strip of burned bacon. Smells like road-dead Possum. Either changes his ways, or she's going to pick up and leave.

Two days later, police escort Marlene to Fairlawns County Hospital for a thirty-day stretch of "Observation and Evaluation."

A young woman arrives with two black eyes, a missing tooth, and a broken nose. Her husband, an amateur boxer, uses her for a punching bag. After his workouts, he orders her to perform oral sex. Suffering from depression, she consults a psychiatrist who prescribes Librium. She attempts to file for divorce, and winds up in Fairlawns instead of court.

Miss Aldridge appears to be daydreaming inside of her glass cage. I knock.

She calls through the intercom speaker.

"Yes, what is it now?"

"I want you to call the police, Miss. Aldridge."

"The police?"

"Yes, I want you to call the police. Have them arrest this woman's husband, lock him up, and let her go home."

Miss. Aldridge opens a chart,(mine, no doubt), and proceeds to scribble. The punching bag remains locked up.

After dinner, I lie upon my bunk, smoking, and trying to plot my escape. With the wind chill factor, the temperature is -30. They've taken our coats, boots, keys, drivers' licenses, and money. I might cut through the wire mesh on the window, but how far would I get in pajamas and cloth slippers? Snow turns to hail, trees sway, limbs crack, Bobby turns over in the top bunk, his bulk sagging inches from my nose.

"Hey there, junior," he says. "What's doin'?"

"Nothing."

"Scared?"

"No."

"'Course you are. But don't worry about that. I'll show you the ropes."

"You've been there?"

"Never have ever. But you stick with old Bobby, you'll do fine."

The siren had gone off right before bedtime, the emergency doors swung open, and the police swarmed over a giant, punching him and trying to kick his legs out from under but he kept swinging. We clapped and cheered. Orderlies tossed a blanket over the big man's head and banged on him with their fists; he roared and laughed and didn't go down. Holding a syringe in each hand, a nurse crept in close, jabbed at a buttock, missed, sprang back and stabbed. The man stiffened, shuffled, wobbled into a crouch and crashed sideways to the floor.

Released from isolation a few days later, Bobby Lee swaggered onto the ward like a champion bull rider at a rodeo. We couldn't wait to hear his story.

"Took a tire iron to old Billy's head," he began. "Happened to be a good buddy a mine. Up 'til then, anyways. Told him afore. Lots a times. 'Billy,' I says, 'now I'm askin' you real nice. Don't want no trouble. But you keep foolin' with my old lady and somebody's gonna get hurt.'

"Man's dumb as a turkey. Plain stupid. Thought I weren't serious but I damn sure was. Crawled under the porch with my dog and a bottle of Jim Beam. Thought they couldn't find me there. But old Jerry, went to high school with that boy, shines his flashlight in there. 'Bobby Lee,' he says, 'you can come on outta there on your own, or we're gonna blow your ass out.' I come out and they threw me right in the drunk tank."

The judge gave Bobby a choice. Two years in the penitentiary or a stint in the snake pit.

"I said, 'Hell no, I ain't crazy. Just had a temper fit, that's all.' Asked that man what he'd do if some hillbilly tried to diddle his own little wife. Pissed him off that did. Said he don't want to hear no more damn nonsense out a me. Ain't got all day, he says. 'Now, what'll it be, boy? Jail or the nuthouse?' Up to you. ' Course I took the nuthouse."

"Tell you right now. Done laid right there on the floor in that dirty old cell. Three days. Wet myself. Guards laughed their asses off. My heart was comin' in by truck, my kidneys by train and my liver by plane. DT's ain't no picnic, folks. Shaking like a chicken with its head cut off. Thought old Bobby was a gonna for sure that time around."

*

Sanity Hearing

I am escorted into a small room where nurses and interns, six in all, are seated around a long shinny table. The chief psychiatrist opens a thick folder. His has long curved banana nose. I want to reach across and peel it. He suffers from dandruff, has yellow teeth, and his hands won't keep still. Everyone knows these "sanity hearings" are a farce. Inmates walk into the hearing room, and three minutes later (we have timed these sessions) they walk out. At Fairlawns County Hospital. Dr. Hendrix is judge and jury. There is no appeal.

He yanks off his glasses, lights a cigarette, blows smoke through his nose and glares at me.

"What time is it?" he demands.

"3:45."

"A.M. or P.M."

Help, he's asking trick questions.

"P.M."

"Where are you?"

Anywhere but here.

"Des Moines, Iowa."

"What's your name?"

Howdy Doody.

I tell him.

"Are you a beatnik?"

I smile.

"Are you a beatnik?" he repeats.

Look at the file, stupid. It's all right there. You keep asking the same old questions, and I keep giving you the same old answers.

"Yes, I am a beatnik."

Once upon a time, I was an ordinary street fighting working class kid. Stole cars. Got drunk. Had sex with my girlfriend in the backseat of a battered '56 Chevy. Acted dumb in school. Sassed my teachers. Got kicked out of class. Played football. Went to church. Couldn't wait to go to war. Drank rotgut in ghetto whorehouses. Had sex with prostitutes, suffered paroxysms of guilt afterward. Accepted my fate — a life of quiet desperation on the "wrong side of the tracks." Got into college instead of state prison. Walked into the world of ideas. Bumped into myself coming out of the dark ages. Soared into a new life; became a huge happy sponge, soaking up art and literature, philosophy and history, psychology and sociology.

Decided that I wanted to be a poet rather than a medical doctor, a clear indication, said my family, that I had gone loony.

Started to wear sunglasses even on dark days; a Greek Air force beret with a beautiful long tassel; blue denim work shirts and flowered ties. Wanted to grow a beard, but didn't have facial hair. Hung out in candle-lit coffee houses with women sporting shades, sandals, and black tights. We listened to Odette and Lead Belly. We read our poetry aloud to jazz, and we said "man," and "cool," and "dig it." We memorized *On The Road*, got drunk, smoked reefer, and recited Howl. We studied the works of Albert Camus, Dostoyevsky, Frederick Nietzsche, Jean Paul Sartre and, proclaiming ourselves existentialists, we intoned, "God is dead. Life has no meaning; therefore, anything is possible."

When we weren't talking about our Egos and Ids and Libidos, we wrote verse poetry and engaged in free love sex. One night, two talented young women writers confided that they were going to tell their parents that they were in love. I urged them to keep their secret. Soon after, these women disappeared.

Dr. Hendrix appears to be in pain.

"Why what?" I say.

"Why are you a beatnik?"

I don't answer.

"Why do you cause so much trouble?"

"What trouble?"

He's turning purple and his head is about to fly off.

"You don't fool me. Ever since you came here, you've been causing trouble. Nothing but trouble."

"Excuse me, Doctor. But what's the point of all this?"

"The point?"

"Why not get it over with. You know you're going to send me to the snake pit."

"Now, you listen here, young man. You are a troublemaker. And in my opinion, you're ninety-five percent sick."

"If I were ninety-five percent sick, I couldn't be having this conversation with you, Doctor Hendrix."

The chief psychiatrist jumps to his feet, crushes his cigarette, and stomps out of the room. I look at my watch. Four minutes, thirty seconds. A record—ninety seconds longer than most Fairlawns sanity hearings.

*

Away

Bobby Lee raises his coffee cup as though he intends to make a toast.

"Come on down, boys and girls," he laughs. "Don't look so damn sad. Ain't no big thing. Junior and I are goin' down to the funny farm. Little vacation that's all. Look out there. Them boys got shotguns just for us. Gonna chain us up like dogs. Well, so long," he sings, "it's been good to know ya. So long, it's been good to know ya. Sorry we just have to be movin' along."

Bobby's right. The deputies carry .12 gauge pump-action shotguns.

Miss. Aldridge brings our coats.

"Now you listen here," she says, handing me a pair of wool mittens. "I don't want to see you around this place again. Do you hear? Don't come back."

I've lost count of the times I've been "observed and evaluated" by staff at Fairlawns. Each time, they administer the same tests— Minnesota Multiple Personality Inventory (MMPI); the Rorschach (Ink Blot) test; the let's move little wooden playschool blocks around test; the "How many times a day do you masturbate?" and "Do you want to make babies with mommy?" and "Would you like to eviscerate your daddy?" tests.

Before I dropped out of college I took psychology classes, so I'm curious to know what label these examiners have assigned to me.

"Do you think I'm schizophrenic?"

"No."

"Do you think I'm a sociopath?"

"No."

"Am I border-line something?

"No."

"Are you a beatnik?" they ask.

"Yes," I laugh, "I am a beatnik. Is that a new mental illness?"

"No, not really."

"Then why does everyone keep asking?"

"It says here in your file..."

"If you can't find a diagnosis for me, then why am I here?"

" Because," they say, "your mother wants you here. She thinks you're sick."

"My mother is crazy."

"She's not here, you are."

"Bring her in and we'll see who needs help."

"We can't do that."

"Why not?"

No answer.

"Wouldn't you like to know if she's lying? She exaggerates everything. Makes up stories. Why do you believe her?"

Silence.

"Don't you think these tests are silly?"

He stares at me.

"Silly."

"Redundant."

"Redundant?"

"Stupid."

On we go, on and on. He opens my file and commences to write. I return to the room where we play board games, smoke, tell stories, and wait for our turn to be escorted to the snake pit.

*

We spin across the meridian into and out of a ditch. Bobby falls forward, striking his head against glass. Blizzard warnings. Schools closed. Events cancelled. Stay off the highways. Wind chill factor –25. No cars on the two-lane road that merges with snow-covered soybean fields. Farmhouses swirl by, smoke floating from their chimneys, people warm and safe inside. The deputies chain smoke and brag about the times they've stopped on the way to the snake pit, yanked crazies out of the car and beaten them with rubber truncheons.

" 'Member that woman wouldn't come outta that shitter. Tried to tell her, didn't I? Thought she's gonna' hide in there. Had to drag her ass out. Use the hose on her. Said her daddy was the president. Man, you liked to kill that crazy bitch, didn't you Ronnie?"

Bobby asks for a cigarette, the deputies oblige. One hand on the wheel, our driver bobsleds down the wrong side of the road.

An apparition looms out of snowbound cornfields. It gets larger and I can't help laughing. Bobby glares at me. "What's so damn funny?" he says.

Brick buildings. Three stories high, with peaked slate roofs and heavily barred windows. A debtor's prison, the poorhouse, an orphanage straight from the pages of *Bleak House*. The deputies stop joking. I feel like a man who, after years of terror, mounts the scaffold, looks out at the crowd, and realizes that it's all an absurd joke. His birth, his life, his crime, and now his death, are a funny mistake.

"This," I say, waving our new home.

"Hell," says Bobby. "Don't look like much to laugh at to me."

"Just Poe," I say.

"Don't know the man," Bobby replies. "Don't care to neither."

Bobby struts through the portals of the snake pit, disappearing down a hallway and I'm taken into a chilly room, ordered to strip naked, bend over and hold my ankles. I obey. A man rams his index finger into me, laughing when I jump with pain. "Nothing up there," he says. He turns on the tap, orders me to sit in a tub filled with tepid water, and hands me a glob of green soap. "Scrub," he says. I shiver, my teeth chatter, and I wonder where Bobby might have gone.

"I'm a drunk," he'll say next time we meet. "Not some crazy nut like you, junior. Got the keys to the kingdom, boy. Me and you'll have a good old time in here. You want uppers, you got 'em. Downers, you got 'em. Get you anything your little heart desires."

My guard lights a cigarette and looks through the barred window. It continues to snow. I curl into myself for warmth. "Get out," he says, handing me a kaki shirt with a number stenciled across the pocket, kaki trousers, and an enormous pair of black work boots. The shirt hangs down to my knees, I clutch the pants to keep them up, and the shoes slip and slide when I walk.

Another man arrives to take me to the barber who runs his electric razor over my skull. Then, a dentist digs into my teeth with a screwdriver-size probe. He jabs and jams, inserts a bit into his drill and proceeds to grind without administering Novocain. Tears slide down my cheeks. I want to scream, but I've made up my mind. I will follow their rules, but I will show them nothing. They can amputate my arm and I won't make a sound. They can scissor my ears off, and I will not react. If they want me to lick the floor clean with my tongue, I'll do that. One way or the other, on their terms or mine, I'm leaving the Snake Pit.

*

Descent

We descend a stairway into a dimly lit tunnel. I shuffle and stumble and trip inside of size-13 shoes. We twist and turn, seem to be retracing our steps, moving deeper into the maze of tunnels that run beneath Moravia State Hospital's gothic buildings. I hear singing. We round a corner and stop at an encampment of six old women and two overgrown children. The campers have spread blankets over the concrete floor. Pots, pans, books, and clothing are scattered across the blankets. A young woman faces her audience. She is beautiful and she is blind. We stop to listen. She sings jazz riffs, swaying to the band inside of her head. She sounds like Ella Fitzgerald, smooth and peppy, shifting from upbeat to melancholy, playing with her own sound. If her lyrics made any sense, she could perform in nightclubs.

"Husband walked out on her," explains my escort. "Shot herself in the head. Didn't die."

We pass other encampments. In one, four old people stare into a bonfire visible only to them. They do not blink or talk or move a muscle when we pass. I wonder if they are mummies. Why are they here in these tunnels? How long have they been in Moravia? Do they have children? Does anyone know they spend their days seated, in silence, rubbing their hands around an invisible campfire?

At last, we enter the ward where I am to be kept. A man with a wide scar running like a tiara across his skull rocks furiously in a large wooden chair. "Saw Hitler," he screams. "Saw Hitler today." He rocks backward, banging his head against the wall, sobbing "Saw Hitler. Saw Hitler. Today. Saw him." A group of men, apparently entranced, gather around a blank television screen. I sit in one of the rocking chairs. Men walk by, stop, stare at me but say nothing. Suddenly, from one end of the ward there's a terrible commotion. A naked boy races through the ward, laughing when an orderly whacks him with a yardstick. Back and forth they go. No one seems to notice.

The boy stops in front of my chair. "Kiss me kiss me kiss me," he screams, climbing into my lap. He presses his nose against mine, stares into my eyes and screams, "Kiss me kiss me." Rearing, he slaps my mouth, leaps to the floor and runs screaming through the ward.

I rock softly in my chair. The men on this ward wear khaki prison clothes, like mine, and huge black clodhopper shoes. Their heads are a patchwork of scars—long, short, wide, thin, odd-shaped, like ink blots, abstract art scars. I imagine Dr. Hendrix in a long white coat, moving an electric saw across a comatose patient's head, exposing brain matter, his assistants probing with ice-pick instruments, searching for the microscopic creatures tucked deep inside of this madman's cerebellum. Dr. Hendrix will be the first human being in history to locate the source of insanity. He will capture these little bastards, put them on display, and be showered with praise and prestigious prizes.

*

On the psychiatric ward of Meredith Hospital, aids strapped me down, dabbed Vaseline on my temples, and put me to sleep with sodium pentothal. They watched a charlatan named Dr. Dash place a spur over my head and flick a switch, running electric current through my skull. My body bucked against the straps and tried to swallow its own tongue. Thirteen violent epileptic seizures, and when it was all over my brain had turned into wet sand. I couldn't read or write poetry, couldn't concentrate or recognize friends and family members.

"Hey," high school buddies would say when they saw me on the street. "How's it going?"

I looked at them.

"Do I know you?" I said. Sometimes, they cried.

Dr. Dash ran from hospital to hospital, shocking depressed, manic, alcoholic, drug addicted, promiscuous, gay, rebellious, eccentric, errant housewives and other uppity people. Dash was protecting society from its deviants, maintaining social order, making sure that people who dared question the way things were, always had been, and always would be were taught to behave. I watched an elderly college professor turn into a drooling child who couldn't figure out how to move his checkers across the board.

*

Questions

He is a small man with a black mustache tiny eyes that crawl about the room, as though searching for a way out of this disheveled chilly office. I shuffle inside, the oversize clodhoppers on my feet like hooves clomp clomping across the floor.

"Sit down," he mutters.

"What?"

"I said sit."

He shuffles a stack of papers, shaking his head to quiet static.

"So, you support Fidel Castro? That right?"

"I support the Cuban revolution."

"Castro's a communist."

"Maybe."

"No maybe about it. He ought to be shot."

"Okay."

"What did you say?"

"I said, 'okay.'"

"Okay what?"

"Okay, go ahead and shoot Castro."

"Why are you here?"

"I don't know."

"I asked you a question."

"Why I'm here?"

"Yes."

The doctor's hands are hairy mittens. He lights a cigarette, inhales, exhales, and taps ashes onto the floor.

"Says you've been in jail."

I nod.

"You quit college."

"Yes."

"Why?"

"Went to San Francisco. Looking for Jack Kerouac."

"Who?"

"Kerouac, Ginsberg, Cassidy."

"You're an alcoholic."

"I like to drink."

"Tried to kill yourself."

"No."

"You used a razor. Tore up your arms."

"Yes, but I didn't want to die. None of us did."

"None of who didn't?"

"The women in Fairlawns."

"You're not a woman."

I start to laugh.

"You know what?"

He stubs out the cigarette, lights another.

I want to tell him that I do not know what. Never met the man.

"I think you're mother's right about you. You're never going to get out of here with an attitude like that. You're going to spend the rest of your life in here. I'll see to that."

*

I sit on the ward, watching Jimmy run from the orderlies. Next to me, a man talks to an invisible companion.

"My problem," he says, "is that I'm a blue blood. My blood is blue. My family has blue blood. That's why I'm here. Why I'm different. I can't help it. It's my blood. It's blue. That's right. I come from a family of blue bloods."

Will I be sent to one of the backwards, stripped, shackled to the wall? Will Dr. Hendrix, followed by a coterie of admirers who want to observe his technique of sawing patterns into human skulls, find me there? Will Dr. Dash arrive with his black box and electric spur, ready to deep fry my brain?

I am here. I will not drink. I will not use drugs or have sex. I will jump out of sleep at 5:00 a.m., make my bed, and line up for breakfast. I will obey every rule, work any job, lick the floor clean with my tongue if ordered to do so.

I plot my escape. One month later the head doctor at Moravia hands me a piece of paper with my name at the top. "This is to hereby certify that on January 30, 1961, the patient was restored to sanity."

I carried that proclamation around for many years on New York's Lower East Side. Sometimes I showed it to people. Everyone thought it was very funny.

φ

FEELING FOR EGGS
Elizabeth Patton

WHEN I THINK ABOUT MY EARLIEST MEMORY, it is always summer, and I am wandering in the yard around the farmhouse. My mother would put me out after breakfast and hook the screened door. I had time and space, but I had to share it with a white leghorn rooster, whose main concern was guarding his property and treating me as a stranger. Once he saw me, he ran toward me, and I ran toward the lot fence. He would spur me if I didn't make it.

One morning he came toward me, and I began running and screaming. My mother ran from the house, yelling at the rooster, but she was also yelling at me. "Stop! Stop! He won't hurt you now." But I wouldn't stop until I made the fence. She pulled me off the boards and ran with me over to the chicken coop. "You stay in here until I come for you." She slid the latch, and I began crying and shaking the door. Nothing gave, and I began to investigate the cracks in the walls.

I heard her screaming, "Get away. Go home. I'll get the sheriff to you." Through a crack I could see that she was standing at the top of the hill, looking down the path through the pecan trees. There was someone coming up fast through the trees. He kept coming, and she kept yelling." Get away from here. I don't want you here."

He gave her a wild look and climbed up on the well frame. He unhooked the bucket and threw it in. Then he began a descent into the water. As he went down, he yelled. She stopped yelling and ran into the house. He kept yelling like nothing I had heard before, long wails that had no end.

When she came back, she stood on the porch, her hands around her elbows, and she was quiet. For a long time there were no sounds but the moaning of the man and the clucking of the chickens around the coop.

I sat down and waited. I wandered around the hen nests. One hen was on the nest. "Good chickie," I said and patted her red feathers. There were some eggs in the nests. I found the basket and began to gather them.

I liked this part of chicken raising. What I didn't like was going under our house to find eggs that the hens dropped. The house was low on rocks in the back and open. I could barely get under to look for eggs. My mother would send me under, and I would fight her. "It's dark under there. I *don't* want to go."

"You'll go. We need those eggs."

Then I would hit her legs, and she would pick me up and shove me under. It was so dark that I would pull myself along with my right hand feeling in front of me. I was so afraid of what might be around me. When I did find an egg, I put it in a pan and dragged it along. "And don't break any." That was the refrain in my mind. Frightened of the dark and the unknown, I could feel my heart. Sometimes there were little noises I didn't want to hear, and my heart beat wildly. Maybe I would find one or two eggs. Those I left would remain secrets.

In the coop I put the basket by the door and sat down on a feedbag. I must have fallen asleep. Sometime later my mother picked me up and took me to the house.

"Where is he?" I asked.

"Who?"

I looked at her and wondered what she had done. Was the man still in the well? I looked at the well and then back at her.

"The man in the well."

"Now, Audrey, there's no man in the well. You had a bad dream. I've told you about going to the coop and staying."

"I got the eggs for you, Mother."

"Thank you, baby. You're a good girl."

I nestled against her, and we went over to the glider and sat for a while.

I never saw the man again. I asked my father about the man in the well, and he told me I must have made him up.

"You know how you make up things, Audrey." I never wanted to go near the well. When I had to, I watched carefully and listened.

Sometime after that day a car came to our house, and my mother left with two men. One was my Uncle Sterling and the other one I didn't know. My father knew him though.

I stayed out in the yard and watched them drive down the hill. Then I wandered out to the washtubs under the big pecan. Asmolia had the fire burning around the big black pot.

"You going to stay with me all day?"

"I guess so. Daddy has gone to work."

"You're in the way now. You go over there and swing."

I went over and began swinging. After a while Asmolia's husband Zark came up. As my swing went their way, I could hear them talking.

"Did she do it?" he asked her. She was bent over the washboard, and I didn't hear what she said. She looked up toward me. "She's a pistol, ain't she?" I thought she was talking about me.

Zark shook his head and moved on to the field. She began pulling sheets out of the pot with a stick and dumping them into the tub. She checked the clothesline and pushed the poles higher before she went back to rinsing.

Then I thought that she was talking about my mother. A pistol, I didn't know any pistol. Maybe she had killed the man in the well. I kept swinging, my legs going higher and higher. Asmolia hung up the clothes. When she finished, she looked up at me. "Come on now, Audrey. Your mama said for me not to let you out of my sight."

"Not now, Asmolia. You stay here with me. I'll let the cat die in a minute."

"You hurry up now. I got to do the house and cook dinner for your daddy. He's coming home today to check on you, and then he's going back to work."

"When's she coming back?"

"I don't know, Audrey. She said, 'Expect me when you see me.' That's all I know."

That night before I went to sleep, my mother came to my room. "I'm back, Audrey. I'll see you in the morning."

As I drifted off, I could hear them talking in the kitchen, but the words didn't make any sense.

"Did he give you any trouble?"

"He was all right, but he cried at the end."

"The surprise of it all, I guess. Did you have any trouble with the car?"

"No, Bruton's car is like ours, only a couple of years older."

"I always think that a Ford will stay with you. A good all-round car."

"You want some more soup, Delbert?"

"No, Asmolia made me a big dinner. The best okra I've had all season."

"Was Audrey all right?"

"Just the same, hanging around Asmolia and in the way. You know how she is on Mondays. You'd think she never had any company."

Monday, washday, Asmolia, swinging, the fire around the pot, a visit from Zark, week after week, and the crying when Asmolia left. "Come back tomorrow," I would plead.

"Now you hush up. I'll be by one day before Monday. You a big girl now, too big to be crying when I leave."

The next morning I asked about the car, but my mother just told me she had to take a trip.

"Was it a Ford?"

"I don't know, Audrey. I never notice cars."

The rooster continued to chase me, and I kept on gathering eggs. The rooster never relented and then began to attack my mother. Not long after one of his most vicious displays, we had chicken for Sunday dinner.

After we ate that day, we took a drive up the Sardis Road. Just across the branch from our house lived Aunt Edith and Uncle Utney. We never saw them except on their place. Sometimes he would sew on a machine out in the yard, but I don't believe I ever saw him sew. I heard that he did. Maybe my mother told me.

"When did she leave?" my father asked.

"Maybe a month ago, I guess," she answered.

"What about Uncle Utney? Where is he?" I wanted to know.

"They both are gone," she answered.

The house had weeds in the yard, and kudzu was covering the barn. I looked hard in case one of them might appear and wave as they used to.

The next afternoon Uncle Sterling and Aunt Sukie came by in their buggy. They were on their way to town.

"Do you need anything?" he asked my mother.

"Can't think of anything."

"Uncle Utney and Aunt Edith have gone away," I said. "We went by there yesterday."

"Is she doing all right?" my mother asked.

"She's with her family over in Vidalia," Aunt Sukie said. "We haven't heard from Utney."

I looked at them carefully. There was something I couldn't understand. Why wouldn't they know about both of them? Did they take the sewing machine with them? I forgot to look. Maybe it was still in the weeds near the house.

Someone rented their farm after a while, and then we moved to town, our farm sold to some people across the river. Asmolia and Zark moved somewhere out of the county.

Aunt Edith and Uncle Utney drifted from mind. We hardly ever saw Aunt Sukie and Uncle Sterling. I never knew who was related to whom until I was grown. I knew that they were my mother's relatives, but no one talked about them.

Years went by, and I came home from college for my mother's funeral. I never knew that she had cancer until my father called to tell me she had died. I took the bus home from the funeral, wondering why everything happened that way with my mother.

A very old couple came to the service and sat near my father and me. "Aunt Sukie and Uncle Sterling," he whispered.

As the service progressed, my mind began to spin around the days when we lived on the farm. I saw my mother in the yard with that white leghorn rooster. I saw her running toward the pecan orchard and heard her screaming at the man. The man in the well. Who was the man in the well? Where did Uncle Utney and Aunt Edith go?

The casket showed my mother as a pretty woman, a woman still young in her forties. I would think of her much later in my life as even younger and stronger.

After the cemetery service we drove back to the house. I asked my father about that day the man came running up to the house and got into the well.

"Uncle Utney had one of his fits, Audrey. Your mother was just trying to protect you."

"He was the man in the well?"

"That's what your mother said. Didn't you see him?"

"I guess so, but I was looking through cracks in the chicken coop. "

He looked puzzled. He didn't seem to understand why I was in the chicken coop. "She said that you were playing in the yard when he came up."

"No, I'm sure of that. I was in the coop the whole time he was there."

A few people came back to the house, a few business people my father knew and come circle friends of my mother. "You poor girl without a mother," they said over and over.

I walked over to Aunt Sukie and Uncle Sterling, who were the only family there.

"What a pretty girl you turned out to be."

"Thank you, Aunt Sukie."

Uncle Sterling looked at me, trying to recognize the little girl in me. "Why, I remember you when that old white rooster used to run you down. He was a mean one. He got so mean that your mama had to kill him.I remember going by to see if she needed anything one day and that old rooster was slung over the clothesline. She had wrung his neck."

"I remember him all right. I was such a little girl that he knew he could hurt me."

I waited for them to say something about my mother, but they seemed interested in their food. I began to think about the man in the well again — Uncle Utney.

"You know, Uncle Sterling, you can clear up something about my mother. Remember that day that you came to our house with another man and took my mother away?"

Uncle Sterling looked at me carefully. "I'll never forget that day. You were just a little bit of a thing then. Asmolia was washing that day, and she took care of you." He looked across the room at my father and then back to me. "I guess you ought to know. Your mama never wanted you to know."

"Know what, Uncle Sterling?"

"That day we took Utney to Milledgeville. We told him we were taking him to Vidalia to visit his in-laws."

"Milledgeville?"

"Your mama and the sheriff and I took him. She drove and we sat in the back seat with him. He was right pleased to be going to Sid's place. He always liked his wife's people, you know."

Aunt Sukie shook her head. "Poor old Utney. He was never crazy. He was just sick. I've said that to Sterling a thousand times. His own brother."

"Your mama should never have done that to him, and to think that I was part of it. The worst thing as I think back was Edith running after the car yelling, 'What did he do? Why are you taking him away?' I looked back and saw her standing out in the road, her apron over her face."

My father came by and stopped. "Have some more food. You people getting caught up?"

"Audrey and I were just talking about the old days," Uncle Sterling said. Aunt Sukie just looked at her food.

My father passed to another group, and Uncle Sterling looked back at me. "The other picture that just won't leave my mind is when we got to the hospital. Utney knew that he wasn't in Vidalia right away. 'This isn't Vidalia. This isn't Sid's place,' he said. Your mother ran in for help while we held him in the backseat. I've thought of that day a lot over the years."

"I would think so. I would think so." I began to think about my mother and wondered how much strength she had needed to drive someone to the mental hospital. She would have been about my age, still young enough to be in college.

"You know, he died there, far away from his family," Aunt Sukie said.

I didn't know that he had died there. I assumed that he and his wife were in Vidalia. My mother must have known.

After people left, my father said that he was glad that I had seen Uncle Sterling and Aunt Sukie. "We didn't keep up with them for years and years. Your mother didn't get on with them. I'm surprised they came."

My father and I didn't say anything much about my mother. We had never talked about her. She always seemed to be around talking to us. We just let her talk, and now we didn't have the habit of talking.

As I took the bus back to school, I tried to think about that day when I saw the man in the well. I didn't ever think that he was Uncle

Utney. I wondered if I could ever have talked with my mother about that day if I had wanted to.

I began to think that I had grown up. I had learned some family secrets my mother would have denied. Perhaps her funeral was the appropriate place to hear them, but I would never know.

As the years have gone by, there are times when I know that I can never forget that little girl, scared, groping in dark spaces, feeling for eggs.

φ

Flying Watermelons
Lawrence Russell

As is true with all successful attempts at banditry, stealing watermelons requires careful planning. A moonless night is essential, as is a thorough attention to the details of the designated attack area. The height of the fence surrounding the field, any significant topographical indentations that might provide cover, and — most importantly — the location and sleep habits of the guard, all have to be taken into account.

The adventurers must never park their vehicle on a paved road near the object field. However slight the chance of raising the suspicion of a passing motorist in the hours shortly after midnight, too many raids have been thwarted by such a careless error, often with the consequence of a load of buckshot in a buccaneer's butt.

The choice of raiding vehicle is also crucial. It must be able to maneuver on rough and unpaved roads and quite possibly across open fields. If a four-wheel drive conveyance is not available, at the least one with reinforced springs and a chassis with a high road clearance is a requisite.

My father owned a pickup truck that met the latter specifications.

Bill, Billy, and I scouted the field on a quiet Sunday afternoon. We found a dirt track — probably an old logging road — leading into a forest of pine and live oak about two hundred yards beyond our target, followed it in a rough line paralleling the field's western fence line, and were eventually able to maneuver the truck to find the northern boundary and bump our way along it to a point of some seclusion beneath a large oak tree. We were pleased to note that we had settled on a spot about as distant from the rough-built guard tower as we could get.

To enable us to return to our point of attack in the dark of the coming night, we blazed a trail on our way out, using a hatchet to make wide slashes in a number of trees. These were not amateurs at work.

There was a tacit understanding between the growers and their menace of teenage bandits that the poaching of watermelons was generally regarded as something of a game, a test of youthful bravado against experienced cunning. As long as there was no wanton destruction of the fruit, and if we attempted to carry off only that needed to sate our immediate appetites, even if we were caught, there was no danger of any punishment, other than notification to our parents. The one exception was what might be administered on the spot by the guard and his twelve-gauge shotgun loaded with buckshot. They were always in play.

Sometime after midnight, under a dark sky made more opaque by massive rain clouds, Bill, Billy and returned to our previously scouted spot and weighted down the top strands of the barbed wire fence with a pair of heavy tree limbs. We could then easily jump over the simple barrier and be on our way.

I was never able to explain this, nor can I today, but something always drew us to the center of the field on these adventures. This was a crop of the Royal Sweet type of melons, described in my grandfather's seed catalog as "....oblong, blocky shaped hybrids with medium dark, fairly wide, green stripes on a light green background, with thick rind and crisp red flesh." I can only assume we believed those with the crispest red flesh were to be found at the innermost part of the patch. Whatever the attraction, that's where we headed, obviously not concerned that every advance took us closer to the guard.

We moved slowly on hands and knees from melon to melon, thumping each to listen for the deep hollow echo that would reveal the ripe fruit. Bill and I each had cut from its vine one of our self-imposed limit of two, and Billy already had a pair, when the searchlight flared on and the shotgun boomed. The buckshot sailed harmlessly over our heads, undoubtedly because that's where the guard had aimed. Bill and I crawled together as fast as we could using what terrain cover was available, until we escaped the light. Then we bounced to our feet and ran pell-mell for the fence.

I looked back once to see an incredible sight. Billy had obviously dropped to the ground like Bill and I when we first heard the shotgun, but he was now back on his feet scrambling to pick up his two watermelons. Bill and I kept going at full speed. We safely cleared the fence, but in doing so, one of us accidentally freed one of the tree limbs, and when it fell, it released enough spring in the barbed wire to fling the second one to the ground as well. The entire fence was then back at its original height.

As Bill and I scrambled into the truck, we looked back to see Billy caught clearly in the bright searchlight. He was running as fast as he could with a watermelon cradled on each shoulder. I swear I heard the guard laugh out loud as he fired the next round of buckshot, a small amount of which caught Billy square in the butt. He let out a yelp, performed a kind of skipping leap, hit the ground back at full gallop, and kept on coming, his watermelons still safely nestled on his shoulders.

Billy never hesitated as he approached the fence. Without breaking stride, he soared over it in a single bound, the watermelons flying right along with him. He gently laid the melons in the back of the truck on the old packing material we had brought along for that purpose and less gently plopped himself in right behind them. And we were off.

Billy later said he didn't mind that we had run without him, but to flee without the melons we had already cut from the vine was inexcusable. It was tantamount to leaving a wounded comrade on the field of battle.

φ

JOHN GREENWOOD
Michelle Brafman

YOU TOLD ME YOU HAD A DREAM about John Greenwood when I called you last month out of the blue to wish you a happy thirtieth birthday. You told me about your big IBM management job and your condo across the highway from Del Mar Beach and your boyfriend. Without words, you told me to archive our college friendship as I would my old prom dress or Barbie's.

You hesitated when I told you that Teddy and I were coming from Chicago to celebrate our fifth anniversary, but I called you back the next day anyway. "Looks like it will be just me," I announced to your answering machine. "Teddy's tied up at work." Truth? Teddy gave me the shoe. Teddy, who massaged my back with olive oil and bought me dark chocolate he couldn't afford when he was a pudgy med student with thinning, mud-colored hair, is sleeping with a lab tech. Fucking cliché. He'll have cleared out his things by the time I return from visiting you.

*

I'm not funny like you are, but you'll laugh when I remind you of the vegan fart. What was that yoga instructor's name? Melody, I think. Worn purple leotard, long gray ponytail, the one who let it rip mid-downward dog. I kept staring at you all beet-faced, biting your cheek, like you were going to lose it any minute. And then you caught my eye, and you snorted, and laughter came out of your throat like a hairball. That finished both of us off.

We relocated our peaceful place against a eucalyptus tree outside the studio, giggling until tears streamed down our faces. "I'm Valerie," I offered between gasps.

"Kat Stramm. Damn glad to meet ya." You held out your hand like you'd just sold me a car, which I found weird, but in a good way.

I shook your sweaty palm. "Melody's totally woo-woo," I proclaimed.

"What's 'woo woo'?" you asked in your Kat manner: Midwestern, earnest, and unafraid to admit that you don't know what something means.

"Like, she's probably really into crystals and tarot cards and stuff. I bet she's a vegan too," I explained, enjoying giving you the lowdown on life in the land of breast implants, Dolphin shorts, and Santa Ana winds. "Vegans only eat veggies," I added with authority.

"Pee-yew, that was some vegan fart she let rip." You plugged your nose and transformed your voice into Melody's throaty whisper. "Let me connect with my chi energy."

I made a mental note to save you a mat at our next yoga class. You were different from any of my high school friends, and it wasn't just because you dressed in those pink polo shirts with the collars turned up, and you pulled your ponytail back so tight that it made your head look like a peeled onion. You used terms like "soda pop" and "bubbler," and you didn't know that listening to Mariah Carey was totally uncool.

We started spending so much time together that it felt funny to walk through campus without you next to me. Scott—I can't believe I went out with him—said you had a girl crush on me, that you watched me like a movie. He was weirded out, but I liked it. I taught you how to roll a joint, shell a lobster, and catch your first wave, which knocked you on your ass.

I borrowed Scott's van and drove us to the La Valencia Hotel. Your eyes frogged out when I let the surfer manager leer down my bikini top. Hell, it scored us access to the finest pool in La Jolla, an order of nachos, and a couple of Diet Cokes. Most men, even the sensitive guidance-counselor types, will do just about anything for a girl with big boobs and blond hair. It's just one of life's ugly truths.

You wore a tank suit, and you kept telling me how lying out in the middle of February made you feel like you were on vacation.

"Put this on. You'll tan faster." I tossed a tube of Bain de Soleil toward your chair and then confided in you about Scott. "He's been acting so needy, you know?"

When you listened to me, I felt like I was whole inside, and not this person who tried to hold it all together with Bubble Yum and Scotch tape. Unlike my mom and my friends, you paid attention instead of waiting for the phone to ring or watching for someone more interesting — a guy — to walk through the door.

"Scott's mother left his dad, moved to Nepenthe to do colonics or grow herbs or something." Actually, my father had left us to grow 'shrooms in Humboldt and fuck fine-boned redheads who looked like my mother, and I was the one who was getting clingy, but I liked this version of the story much better, and you were buying it.

*

I was stoked when you invited me to Milwaukee for Easter. I'd traveled outside of California once, but I'd spent hours of my childhood watching *Happy Days* reruns on Nickelodeon, and I pictured your life as some version of Richie's: the pot roasts, the bubbly smiles, and the stern but knowing lectures Howard gave Richie when he succumbed to the Fonz's influence. I envied Fonzie's luck in scoring a garage apartment over the Cunninghams' perfect little world.

On the plane ride to your house, we downed Frescas and little bags of honey-covered peanuts while I told you how my new boyfriend, Hugh, was nothing like Scott. You admitted that you liked Hugh's roommate John Greenwood, and I started hatching a plan right then to hook you two up.

Your mother greeted us at Mitchell Field dressed in size 12 mom clothes: pearl earrings, navy blue slacks, and a greenish blue sweater set that matched the color of her eyes. She probably never snuck into your closet and stretched out the waistbands of your miniskirts.

"Girls! Welcome!" She gave us a perky hello and then kissed you on the forehead.

"Hello, Mrs. Stramm." I stuck out my hand like you did the first time we met.

"Nice to meet you." She didn't even try to pretend she wasn't checking out the island of flesh between my T-shirt and my jeans. You pivoted around on your heel, away from your mother and toward me, so that we stood shoulder to shoulder. I was touched by your protectiveness, but your mom didn't bother me; women checked me out more than men did. I just wanted her to like me. I wanted a mom who would pick me up at the airport or a school play or at least my graduation. You didn't get how lucky you were.

Your white colonial with the big garage really did look like the Cunninghams' house. You found Milwaukee's gray spring skies and brown grass depressing, but the sun wears out its welcome when it shines three hundred sixty-four days a year. Your house smelled really good, like vanilla and ham. I loved looking at all those framed pictures of you guys on ski trips, at swim meets, and smiling in your matching Christmas sweaters. You looked like your dad — the same narrow hips, broad shoulders, high forehead, and milky brown eyes — and your cheerleader sister resembled your mom. Perfect little family; each kid gets a parent to favor.

The next morning, I told you I didn't want to go to the mall because I had a headache, but I really wanted to stay home and scallop potatoes with your mom. My mother had me when she was twenty, and she treated me like I was one of her pals. She was fun sometimes, but I hated hearing about what an asshole my dad was for leaving her with a five-year-old. I hated shopping with her for her push-up bras and spending holiday dinners eating greasy egg rolls with one of her bosses, typically a lawyer with a fake tan and gelled-up hair who wanted to sleep with her and maybe even me too. Gross.

Your mom gave me the stink-eye for showing up at your table wearing a tube skirt and white pumps. You told me later that my courage to wear those shoes inspired you to thumb your nose at your mother's No Whites Before Memorial Day rule. My mother never told me about any such rule. My outfit made me feel trashy.

"Here you go, Valerie." Your father, who looked like Roy Clark with his broad, wide-open face, served me the best piece of ham. I still drool when I think of your mom's cake: coconut smothered in fluffy chocolate frosting, decorated with pink, violet, and white jellybeans.

"This little confection is Kat's favorite." Your mom looked at you with something like awe, and you warmed to her affection, like you were her kitten and she'd just scratched you under the chin. "Here's to another semester of straight A's." She raised her wineglass.

"Here, here." Your dad clanked his beer mug against your mom's glass and grinned at you.

"Kat's a total brain," I chimed in.

We were all basking in the glow of this Richie Cunningham family moment when your mother did a weird thing that was seismic, yet so subtle that I wasn't one hundred percent sure it really happened. You cut a second piece of cake for me, and then, just as you were about to cut one for yourself, your mom said, "Kat!" like she would if you were about to walk in front of a car or step on a piece of glass. Then she ran her perfectly manicured index finger along the side of her face.

I had no idea what the hell that meant, but you did. You sat there frozen, as if someone had removed your battery. And then you finished cutting the cake, but you only took one bite, your lip slightly quivering. She'd gotten to you.

*

After we finished up the dishes, we went outside and smoked a joint I'd smuggled from San Diego in a Band-Aid box. We waited until the house was dark before we snuck down to the basement and watched reruns of *The Bob Newhart Show*. "Good thing you're here. I'd be so busted for eating my mom's secret stash of chocolate." You pulled a bag of M&Ms from your mom's needlepoint bag and popped four into your mouth. "You know what chocolate does to the skin, dear?" Your voice took on your mother's high pitch.

"Your skin is fine." I used my "telling it like it is" tone that made you believe anything I said.

"Tell her that," you spat, surprising me with your anger. "She still treats me like the poster child for tetracycline."

"That's fucked up." I shook my head. I felt like I was going to cry; pot made me like that sometimes, but being around you and your mom was making me ache a little too.

We lay on our backs crunching M&Ms, and then you rolled on your side and rested your head in the crook of your arm, and I did the same. I could smell the M&Ms on your breath. You told me that you never talked about your mother to anybody, and I said the same thing, and then we spent the next four hours analyzing our moms, swabbing open wounds, fingering each other's hearts.

I told you about the time I was six—the year after my dad left— and I overheard the dentist yelling at my mother for letting me suck myself to sleep with bottles of apple juice. She had to grovel to my dad for money to pay the dental bill, which he gave, but then he didn't visit us for a long time because he said he couldn't afford it. We lay there draped over those beanbag chairs, the air thick with confession, and then we went into the bathroom, cracked a window, and took a few more hits off my joint.

I turned your shoulders around toward the full-length bathroom mirror and unbuttoned your preppy little pastel yellow Oxford shirt. "Do you know how many people would kill for this?" I ran my hand along your taut skin, and we both stood there for a second admiring your flat belly. Our eyes locked, and I cradled your delight at this new way of seeing yourself. I don't think I wanted anything else to happen, but I felt closer to you than I ever had to any guy.

The spell was broken by the sound of your dad's heavy footsteps padding around the linoleum kitchen floor overhead.

"Midnight snacker." You pointed toward the ceiling, and we cracked up.

"I'm going to talk to Hugh about John Greenwood when we get home."

"Valerie! God, I should never have told you about that." You covered your face with your hands, but I could tell that you were psyched.

You snored like a truck driver while I lay in your guest bed, composing my pitch to John Greenwood, savoring the feel of your mom's three-hundred-thread-count Laura Ashley sheets against my skin. I started thinking about the things I'd told you and the things I never could, like how on my eighth birthday, my father popped back into my life. He showed up holding a silver Daffy Duck Mylar balloon and a box of stale caramel corn in his slender, almost womanly hands. He drove me up to Grauman's Chinese Theatre in his orange Karmann Ghia to see *Bonnie and Clyde*, and then I sat in the car and sipped warm grape Fanta left over from the movie while he dropped off a brown paper bag at a UCLA frat house. Homegrown mushrooms. I felt like Faye Dunaway.

Later that night, my mom's headboard clanked against the paper-thin walls that separated our bedrooms, and when it finally stopped, I heard my father tell her that he still loved her. He snuck out of the apartment before the sun came up, before I got to say goodbye or thank him for the balloon. Not until I entered the third grade did I stop listening for him, waiting for him to sneak back, worrying that I'd miss him if I closed my eyes for even a second.

I couldn't tell you that I missed the first day of third grade because I sat in the stuffy beige waiting room of a clinic while my mom corrected an "oops." The toothy receptionist handed me a cherry Lifesaver that tasted like her patchouli oil. I sucked on it while I read pamphlets about birth control methods and sexually transmitted diseases and tried to forget about how much I wanted a baby sister. It was hard enough taking care of my mom and myself.

And then I replayed what your mom did to you with the cake. The cake that she'd so carefully decorated with jellybeans. Pink, violet, white, pink, violet, white. It must have taken her an hour to line them up so straight. I tried to chase away the black ugliness that threatened to eat up every ounce of sympathy I'd felt for you while we were lying on those beanbag chairs. Up until that night, I'd assumed that I was a novelty to you, that you'd figure out I was just the face of Southern California and not strong and real and grounded. You'd move on someday, because you could, and there'd be nothing I could do to keep you. But that night your mother marked a trail to a place inside you, tender and powerless. A place I could grab hold of and give a good squeeze.

On the flight home, we watched a bad Kathleen Turner movie while we ate airplane lasagna and tried to find comfortable spots on our earlobes for our headphones. You ran your hand over your cheek, and it reminded me of an article I'd once read about an amputee, a Vietnam vet who went insane trying to scratch an itch on his missing limb. Relieved that my bad feelings from the night before had vanished, I elbowed you too hard in the ribs. "You're not that girl anymore. You're very pretty." And you looked back at me with gratitude and more love than had ever come my way.

*

I acted like I did you a big favor by getting John Greenwood to ask you out, but he would have anyway. Everyone loved you. Unlike me, you have this way of inspiring people to be the best version of themselves when they're around you. I still make people uncomfortable, even when I try not to.

"Makeover time," I announced when I showed up the next day with a bag full of clothes from Contempo Casuals. Did you think I had the money to buy that stuff? I shouldn't have accepted your money to pay for it, but I knew that your parents sent you checks for "little pick-me-ups," so I figured it all evened out somehow.

You ripped off your T-shirt from some swim meet and slid on a new milk chocolate brown Esprit sweater, the first of many that you'd buy because the color generated so many compliments on your eyes. You were about to go out on a date with John Greenwood, campus hunk, wearing a pair of white-hot jeans and bikini underpants. I'd renovated your look, big time.

The night of your date, I slept at Hugh's house so I could wait up for John and get the dirt. I was planning to dump Hugh. He was demanding and boring, and we started to fight about stupid stuff — he even told me that he was jealous of you. I hated his weakness. Weak men bail. By then, I was already massively flirting with Jack, my sociology T.A., who rode a motorcycle and gave really good phone. He seemed strong, too. Solid.

I drifted off before John came home, but I slept poorly that night. I blamed it on Hugh invading my space. By morning, I couldn't wait to see you. Part of me wanted John to like you, because I thought that would make you happy; but if you fell in love, I'd have to share you. It never occurred to me that I had overlooked another possibility entirely.

I waited outside your dorm in Hugh's VW Bug for fifteen minutes, agitated as hell until I spotted you behind the big glass door. How could I ever have been annoyed with you? But when you moved toward me with an extra sway in your hips and your shoulders pulled back straight, instead of your usual hunching to make them appear smaller, I felt something turn over inside of me.

You plopped down next to me in a crewneck T-shirt dress that would have made me look lumpy. That thought never even crossed my mind when I shoplifted it for you.

"You're glowing," I told you as I pulled away from the dorm.

"He's nice," you answered in this neutral way.

A vague ugliness swirled around in my stomach. "You don't seem psyched."

"He smells like feet." You sounded so fucking coy.

"Gnarly." I tried to come off lighthearted, but my anger spread through my body like that case of crabs that infiltrated our dorm, when we got back from Easter break.

"Watching a geriatric Ruth Gordon frolic in bed with a college kid didn't have an aphrodisiac effect on us." You were trying to sound so sophisticated, Ms. Cheesehead. I wanted to smack you.

"He talks about boring stuff, and he's kind of self-absorbed," you went on.

I wanted to ask you if you knew a nineteen-year-old guy who wasn't.

"I'll give him another try, but I'll probably end up giving him the size seven-and- a-half narrow. Total shoe." You used my phrase, or your phrase you made up to describe my breakups.

We didn't talk much during the rest of the ride; I pretended I was concentrating on the winding road leading down to the La Jolla cove. The perv manager brought us a few orange juices, and we picked hearty, expensive lounge chairs on the terrace overlooking the ocean. I leaned back, closed my eyes, and concentrated on the hot San Diego sun and the sound of the waves lapping against the rocks. And then a fat man with a farmer's tan jumped into the pool, splashing both of us, and we started laughing, trying too hard to recapture the vegan fart experience. A nagging thought insinuated itself into my pores: you had chosen to stay single over dating a campus babe.

*

I couldn't even face you for a week, so I told you that Hugh and I were going through something really intense when I finally showed up at your dorm room with a bag of Mint Milanos, two Cokes, and one of Hugh's homegrown joints. We sat on your skinny little bed, smoked the whole thing, and acted out the words to a Men at Work song about a Vegemite sandwich. You laughed, and I joined you, not even because anything was funny. We were just high and happy to be back in our groove.

And then I noticed a card on your desk, some stupid Boynton card with a cat holding a bouquet of balloons, and I knew John Greenwood had sent it, even before I read it when you went to pee. All those bad feelings from our conversation about your date came back.

"I'm so glad I cheered you up, Kat."

You just kept laughing because you didn't understand what I was saying.

"Even if we needed a little help." I put my index finger and thumb together and inhaled on an imaginary joint. "Don't worry about John. He's a jerk anyway." I couldn't look you in the eye and lie, so I dropped my gaze and concentrated on prying open the two halves of my Milano. "He told Hugh he met someone else." Actually he'd confessed sadly to me that you weren't into him, but I couldn't stop lying to you even if I wanted to. You looked like you did Easter night when you served us that second piece of cake, when your mom showed me how to douse your battery.

I hugged you hard, and eventually we both passed out on your mildewy dorm carpet. I felt like crap the next day, but I couldn't apologize to you or tell you how scared I was that one day you'd "John Greenwood" me, so I took you to a hair salon where I sat cross-legged on a black leather swivel chair and watched Cassandra, my anorexic hairdresser, chop off your ponytail in exchange for fifty dollars I'd swiped from Hugh. When Cassandra finished, I placed my index finger on your jaw and moved your head from side to side. Your new wisps rounded out the corners of your square face. Lovely. "The bangs totally work," I told you. Your eyes filled with pleasure at your new face, and in the mirror we held that look for the fastest few seconds of my life.

*

When I called to wish you a happy birthday, did you tell me that you'd dreamt about John Greenwood for a reason? Did you ever discover my lie? It doesn't matter because once I knew I could get inside of you, I just kept doing it until you started to hate me more than you loved me. You didn't come to my wedding — it conflicted with your sister's — and you were living in Tokyo when my mom died. Pancreatic cancer. You sent a handwritten note; your mother probably taught you how to write such notes.

Now you've come directly from the office to meet my plane. You're wearing an expensive brown suit. Good color. You no longer slouch, and your legs are bare and toned. You look fabulous.

I slide into the leather passenger seat of your new Audi; my skin soaks up the moist sea air. You chatter on about office politics, and you tell me how your boyfriend proposed at Joshua Tree after he arranged with your boss to kidnap you one afternoon last fall. I try to anchor myself in your long Midwestern a's and o's, and I want to ask if you still travel to Chicago for business and why you don't call when you're in town. I want to siphon just a little bit of your strength; you won't even miss it. Instead, I suggest that we sit on the deck of the La Valencia later on and drink gin and tonics. I miss the waves, I tell you, but I also wonder if the surfer manager still works there and whether or not he would even recognize us. Well, actually me.

I ponder how many drinks it will take before I tell you about Teddy, if you'll listen to me attribute his leaving to some incident I've mined from his childhood to help corroborate my story. You do that well.

We drive along the coast to your tidy condominium complex. You live east of I-5, easy access to newly minted strip malls filled with gorgeous produce and frozen yogurt shops. I could never live in a development of people who share my floor plan, but you can, so I compliment you on scoring a condominium with an ocean view, albeit somewhat obstructed. Then I ask for a shower.

There is no black mildew trapped in your bathroom tiles. I squeeze the bottle of your expensive apricot shampoo until the orange liquid runs through my fingers, and your hard-earned IBM dollars slide down the drain. I don't even wash my hair. I fold myself up in a thick blue towel, the kind I remember from visiting your family that Easter. Your mother probably sent it as a housewarming gift.

You've pushed together a row of power suits swathed in dry cleaning bags to make room for me to hang my clothes in your guest closet. I pick a pale blue suit that matches the color of my eyes, tear the thin layer of plastic from the hanger, and hold the raw silk against my naked body. It kisses my breasts like a cat's tongue, soft and scratchy.

Nordstrom. Size six. I slip my arms through the jacket and watch my damp hair leave a dark ring around the neckline. I picture you wearing this to your executive meetings or to "sit-downs" with employees whose performance has waned. Where would I ever wear a suit like this? Not to the trendy Lincoln Park cafe that I've been managing for the past six years, first to help put Teddy through school, now because I'm not sure what else to do. I am in the midst of tugging the skirt over my hips — bare, white, and too fleshy for the V-string panties drying on your laundry rack — when you catch me trying on your clothes, your life.

I charged a $349 airplane ticket I couldn't afford for the chance to laugh over the vegan fart and breathe in the sweet mediciney scent of eucalyptus, but the words escape my lips before I can stop them. "Jeez, Kat, this looks like something your mom would wear."

Your anger I might be able to handle, but you avert your eyes quickly and with kind pity. "I'm running out for some limes." And then you disappear, leaving me in your ill-fitting skirt and my naked shame.

You're pouring tequila into a blender when I finally emerge from your guest room. We wait until we've settled ourselves into your new deck chairs before we drink. Through an opening between two white stucco buildings, I see a sliver of blue ocean. A sailboat glides across the crack, and it reminds me of when I stood on the deck of a rented Cal 25 and flung my mother's ashes toward Coronado. Funny thing — I don't remember the color of the sky, or the sound of the seagulls, or the feel of Teddy's hand. I only remember thinking that nothing could hurt worse than losing you.

φ

DETROIT
Edward Perlman

Back then, I used to wonder what was it
that Ford and Chevy put into the paint
to make the cars appear internally lit

as if by fire. I mastered self-restraint
in parking lots where summer's shimmering rays
of heat intensified the glow. A faint

aura, a vibration over a hood, a haze
above a trunk, could singe me with desire
I knew I dare not satisfy. I'd gaze

upon aquamarine with my entire
will bent on keeping hands from skimming across
a shimmering fin. Whenever I'd admire

a star-mist blue or moon-flecked midnight moss,
I'd clench my fists in pockets. I used to keep
eagle's eyes out for candy-apple gloss

and vermilion phoenix fire; I longed to leap
into the paint, to swim in the infinite
beneath the surface, to feel the red down deep.

φ

IF, THEN, BUT
FIVE PIECES IN THE STYLE OF KAFKA'S "UP IN THE GALLERY."
George Nicholas

1.

IF, BY SOME CHANCE, I SHOULD RUN across your diary one day while cleaning, a diary I never knew existed, and I should pick it up to admire its hand-tooled red leather cover, to move it from the desk-top I am about to polish, and in that act drop it to the floor where it opens to a page where I can clearly see my name written and so am compelled, with fear and trembling, to read and learn that all is well, you love me, are forgiving of habits that would vex anyone—should that occur I would then be the happiest of men, yet filled with shame over my deed and mourning over the fact that I would never be able to share with you what I had learned, fearing it would break the perfect structure I now truly know we had created.

But instead I know of no such book and imagine that if it did exist you would there deposit all your feelings of being trapped and neglected, stymied and bored, feelings of not being loved fully enough, psychically and physically; instead I am glad that no such book exists atop this table for fear of its contents, yet saddened that there is not enough passion to create it, so I yearn for a secret that is not to be.

2.

If I went to the pound and rescued a dog from lethal injection, thereby securing his loyalty to me forever, and gave you this dog from death row who would tell me of your every move and let me into your house to place flowers on your mantelpiece—not roses, but ginger and irises and tulips—and gifts of chocolate on your bedside table and take with me as I leave the smell of your pajamas hanging in the closet; and if this dog would growl at other suitors and lead you, on your walks, to my front door where he would signal me with a lilt of a floppy ear of your mood that day and how to cheer you and how to make you forget other men with rough hands and sinewy arms, then you would have the time to learn about my own buried charms.

But instead this dog would become your dog and bare his teeth to me if I came round, or would never be housebroken so that for the rest of your life when you smell dog piss you think of me.

3.

If some professional criminal were to approach me for access to the records of the company at which I work in order to transfer enormous amounts of money to a Swiss bank account—no, two Swiss accounts, one for him and one for me — and I agreed, I know that I would be successful only for a short time, despite my discipline to not spend the money for fear of attracting attention (all the while secretly thrilling at its enormity) or perhaps despite my immediately fleeing to a remote part of the world without extradition where I would be the richest man for miles in all directions and from where I would send postcards of palm-backed beaches, e-mails with links to photos of my villa, FedEx letters with hard-copy first-class tickets in your name (no strings attached explicitly stated) and still you do not come, forcing me to return home to see you, leading to my immediate capture and imprisonment, then so respected would I be by the other inmates (and ultimately you—finding an essence of me in chains that you could not discern while I was soaring) that the prison years would pass in serene contemplation, meditation, and profound personal growth, the recognition of which would cause you to wait for my release.

But instead, no professional thief calls me, and even if one did, I would feel the blood run from my face and the sweat form on my very cold forehead and the thought of prison would not conjure visions of serene contemplation, and when I decline the offer and hang up the phone, I would then live in anxiety of the day when I hear that, indeed, the embezzlement has occurred and will wonder which of my timid compatriots took the call (maybe even you?) and if someone out there thinks I may know too much.

4.

If I were to notice you at the seashore lying on a towel, most of you exposed to the sun, yet so blatantly self-contained that only the blind would dare approach you, then I could prove my understanding of your completeness, of the internal you, by ignoring your supine self—not even looking—and thereby gaining your respect to such a degree that you would pursue me and, having caught me, yield to me.

But I find you here before me at a food court, and you are fully clothed and I am devouring you with my eyes, I cannot stop, and you have called your boyfriend over, who has thrown my food in the trash and still I look past him and through your clothes and it is wonderful despite both the approaching fist and the approaching security guard, the latter of which will arrive, alas, second.

5.

If some preternaturally robust ovoid filled with hydrogen and powered by two Rolls Royce engines attached to its double-wide-trailer-sized gondola were to drag its tether through my fallow field as I contemplated whether to plant soybeans or corn come the spring, momentarily blotting out the winter sun while screams of passengers rain down like audio graupel, and one voice in particular—yours—rouses me to leap over hedgerows, catch the tether in my teeth and solidly anchor it to the pickup reel of my John Deere 630 rigid cutting platform combine; and if that tether straightened so that all the gondola occupants could slide safely into my arms—gently, gently, as I avert my eyes from inside the billowing skirts of the ladies, even yours, which I admit to imagining so often in these very fields when on humid summer nights and unable to sleep I have come to count the stars, but instead see your shape in the heavens as I lie awake and aroused to no good end—then not only would everyone wave when I got my coffee at Earl's the next morning, but you would invite me to sit at your table there and later in the kitchen of your parent's home.

But instead the ovoid is merely an ad with cameras, slowly and uneventfully making its way to float above the Ohio State Buckeyes homecoming game against the Wolverines of Michigan.

φ

THE END OF THE SEASON
Susan McCallum-Smith

SHE REQUESTED THAT THE VISITOR be shown into the drawing room while she finished a letter. After tidying her writing desk, she patted her gray hair and smoothed the front of her stiff black gown before heading downstairs.

Had Mrs. Charles Merrick been willing to examine her feelings, she would have realized that she had been expecting this visit, and that she was relieved, relieved in the way that someone gravely ill must be relieved to know that one is, in fact, dying, and that suffering from uncertainty has ceased.

In the drawing room, cream linen shades blotted the thick New York summer. At first Mrs. Merrick could not see her, because her visitor skulked in a corner where shadows clustered as though ashamed. Then the woman startled as if she had been caught doing something uncouth. Her hands were fisted over the porcelain handle of a fragile parasol.

"Why, Miss Parker," said Mrs. Merrick. "Sarah, my dear."

Mrs. Merrick beckoned the younger woman toward her. Miss Parker hesitated momentarily then succumbed. Their bustles crackled like kindling as they wove, hand-linked and cautious, between spindly tables to stiff chairs before an unlit fire.

Miss Parker's face was flushed. Perhaps it was the heat, perhaps the flurry of her hansom cab ride, trying to protect the pale lemon silk from smudges or her brown eyes from being caught by the glance of a stranger, or perhaps it was the daring of her enterprise, for a single young lady traveling alone outside of the acceptable calling hours was apt to stain more than a dress.

"Mrs. Merrick," she began, "I didn't mean to disturb you." She perched on the edge of the chair. Unsure where to put her parasol, she propped it against a side table, her hand hovering in front of it as if it, or she, might fall. "Whatever must you think of me?"

"I don't know what to think of you, my dear," Mrs. Merrick replied. "As I've yet to discover why you are here." This remark was naked of the customary obliqueness but adorned by Mrs. Merrick's high smile. Miss Parker paused as though scolded. Mrs. Merrick leaned forward, causing her bodice to creak.

"It's always a pleasure to see you," she said, "Nevertheless."

The room was comfortable and ornamented with trumpet lilies and Chinese vases, Russian lacquer boxes and Baedekers, all the accumulated bric-a-brac of Mrs. Charles Merrick's celebrated stylishness. Miss Parker, however, ignoring the trinkets around her, concentrated on arranging her dress, as if gathering her thoughts in its folds.

Mrs. Merrick watched the young woman's tentative steps toward the hazardous waters of conversation and decided to plunge in ahead.

"I should have moved on to Newport, you know," she said, "now the season is over." She fingered the jet strands at her neck. "It is only by good fortune that you caught me."

She waited patiently. No, a little impatiently — for the other woman to leave shore. Miss Parker appeared unwilling to join her. "Are you in any trouble, my dear?"

Miss Parker shook her head vehemently, then drew a breath and leapt in. "I wanted to offer my condolences," she said, "on the death of Mr. Merrick's father."

Mrs. Merrick glanced sideways at the marble mantelpiece where the more conventional condolences were arrayed, elegantly scripted and messenger-delivered, trimmed in black ribbon and devoid of the awkwardness of authorial accompaniment. Her gaze slipped back to Miss Parker, who smiled — a smile too broad for elegance, though one had to concede that her teeth were good.

"My husband is at his business premises this afternoon," said Mrs. Merrick. "Something or other about the railway." She twitched her shoulders to indicate her indifference to those masculine concerns. "Normally he is home at this time."

"I know," said Miss Parker.

I know she said. Not *Is he* or *I see*, but *I know*. It was enough. At last, Mrs. Merrick, too, knew. She knew, at last, who and what she was dealing with and the anguish of searching through her broad circle of acquaintances and along the broad avenues of upper Manhattan was over. She felt relief, relief flavored with hard, black anger.

She looked at Miss Parker's face, at the attempt to hide fear and perplexity behind a rosy insouciance, and her mind sailed back over thirty years of other young women fluttering like moths on other sofas and armchairs in New York, Rhode Island or Bar Harbor, young women who had shared that same youthful vitality along with that same naïve expression until the sudden comprehension of the rules of the society in which they lived had passed over their faces like night, for Mrs. Merrick had often felt obliged to inform them of the bleaker realities, the unbearable demands of loyalty, the stultifying disease of boredom, and the slippery nature of reputation, obliged because her husband walked through their dark world like light, and as she pondered her choices, entrapment or release, Miss Parker trembled in front of her, flimsy and yellow, on the starched Austrian brocade, and she realized, with a slight surprise, that she wanted to tell this particular young woman to leave. It would be the kindest thing to do. But why be any kinder than had she had been to all the rest?

"You must stay until my husband comes home," said Mrs. Merrick. "You will keep me company."

Miss Parker blinked.

Mrs. Merrick waited in vain for a flurry of excuses, for surely the young woman would flee? She would flutter and bat against the window shades, the picture rails, and cornice, hurl dizzily beneath the Tiffany glass. All the expensive bric-a-brac would be vulnerable to her attempt. Instead she sat silent, forcing Mrs. Merrick to deal with the repercussions of her choice. Mrs. Merrick leaned over and pulled the crimson bell rope by the fireside. "You know my husband was a great admirer of your father," she said.

An unfortunate subject but the first that came to mind. Charles Merrick and Fitzgerald Parker had gone into business together many years before, but Charles had succeeded where Fitzgerald had failed, as Fitzgerald had been kind but foolish. Since then Fitzgerald Parker had died leaving Sarah Parker and her mother to begin their descent from respectable society, slowly dispensing the last of his income and unable to work or claim kinship with any of the old New York families, as they were Illinois born.

A maid appeared in the doorway.

"We shall have some tea, please, Rosie," said Mrs. Merrick. She turned to her guest, who gazed at her hands on her lap. "No—I think some tea for me and some lemonade for Miss Parker." The young woman glanced up. "You look at little flushed, my dear."

The maid's skirts could be heard sweeping down the hallway. Outside the long windows a few carriages trundled by, the dense air muffling hooves and wheels like eiderdown. Mrs. Merrick sifted through various topics to keep the conversation afloat.

"Are you and your mother still living in that charming little house on 14th Street?"

"Yes."

The brownstone was tethered to the stern of the fashionable neighborhoods like a small launch. As more waves of immigrants arrived and society moved farther uptown, Mrs. Merrick knew that the brownstone and its occupants would eventually be cast adrift.

"And I understand you were in the whirl of the season." Mrs. Merrick was swimming resolutely now. "Though, if I may, I'd like to offer a little advice and say you must be more careful about which invitations you accept."

She suspected that Miss Parker was used to advice. Mr. Merrick had always been very free with it. Miss Parker had probably attended many of the best society events, or maybe not the best for she was young and how was she to know, but Mr. Merrick would certainly have secured her invitations to those functions where he might enjoy her company. Mrs. Merrick, so familiar with her husband's machinations, had convinced herself that it was the boring predictability of his deceit that provoked the greatest bitterness, rather than the fact of it.

"And," Mrs. Merrick concluded with another high smile—as though this were the solution to everything—"we must find you a good husband, my dear."

Mrs. Merrick was denied the pleasure of a response by the entrance of the maid carrying a tray bearing tea and a crystal pitcher of lemonade. The maid placed it on a table between them. Mrs. Merrick poured lemonade into a glass and handed it to Miss Parker. It was opaque yet tangy, like sunlight without heat, and Miss Parker gulped it down, spilling a little on her dress. Mrs. Merrick kindly averted her gaze.

The French clock kept languid but remorseless time, while Mrs. Merrick persevered. She talked of art exhibitions and charity events and considered the merits of various respectable bachelors between the ages of twenty-five and fifty, dismissing or approving each in turn until eventually her words dribbled to drops like the dregs at the end of a glass and the two women sat drained and oddly becalmed.

The front door slammed in the hall. Miss Parker flinched and put her glass on the tea tray with a clatter. Mrs. Merrick remained where she was, one hand under her saucer, the other hanging limp over the side of her chair. The room had darkened so much during their strange vigil that Mrs. Merrick's mourning dress had receded into the shadows and she sensed her resemblance to the Rembrandt that hung on the wall behind her, all ash and pale skin, indefinable outlines and inscrutability. She regretted her decision.

Footsteps echoed in the hall. An exchange of voices. Somewhere, a door closed. Mrs. Merrick pulled the crimson rope.

"Please tell Mr. Merrick to come to the drawing room," she said, when the maid arrived. "I have a surprise for him." She tilted her head toward Miss Parker. "He'll be so pleased to see you."

Miss Parker's hand hovered to one side as if reassuring herself of the location of her parasol. Her eyes were damp and blank.

Mrs. Merrick composed her features, rehearsing her lines for the coming charade. She studied the woman pinned to the chair opposite her, at the yellow satin ribbon binding the young thin neck and felt her resolution falter. Miss Parker's pulse beat rapidly beneath the freckles of her modest décolletage and the rosy glow had faded from her cheeks, leaving the tip of her nose bright red. Mrs. Merrick wanted to say something but she was so used to not saying what she meant that the demands of truth seemed beyond her.

"Miss Parker," she said. She paused, looked at the empty hearth, tugged at the cuffs of her gown and began again.

"Sarah," she said. "Although my husband is generous with his affections, his memory is short and it would be unfair of me, or anyone else, to demand too much from him." The honey particles of dust swirling in front of the window shades appeared to buoy her words up in the air. Miss Parker's eyes locked on hers. "I do hope, my dear, you have not been so foolish as to have believed everything he said."

Miss Parker's hands flew to cover her face. Mrs. Merrick stretched across the tea table and caught them in her own. Waves of comprehension and sympathy washed over the two women and they clung to one another, speechless, to save themselves from drowning.

The drawing room door opened. Miss Parker emitted a slight gasp, dropped Mrs. Merrick's hands, and sprang to her feet. Her bustle clipped the tray and toppled a sugar bowl to the floor. It bounced, unheeded, on the Oriental rug in a soft billow of crystals.

Charles Merrick stood in the doorway, his expression impassive, and one hand resting on his necktie. At the sight of her handsome husband, Mrs. Merrick pulled back from the truth and straightened her spine. A resigned smile played lightly on his lips, as he briefly acknowledged Miss Parker's presence with a swift nod in her direction without taking his eyes from his wife's face. Then he slipped his other hand into a trouser pocket and jingled some coins, like a gambler who has just lost a round of cards but is calculating whether he has enough left to risk another bet.

This gesture streamed over Mrs. Merrick like cold water and she saw him, as if for the first time. She noted the casual elegance of his stance, the complacent confidence in his wrinkled yet boyish face, and his complete disregard for the pretty prey that stood quivering between them, and she knew he was relying on her to finish the game with the same innate sense of propriety she had shown in the past.

She rose and slipped one arm around the young woman's slim waist.

"Is it not astonishing, Charles," she said, "that Miss Parker should cross New York, all alone, and on such a day, just to call on people like us?"

φ

AT THE DANCE
Ru Freeman

MY FATHER HAS A BEARD and I am not attracted to bearded men. I do not think of E, therefore, until I overhear the *white* girls talk. Their enthusiasms break around me and I sit up, suddenly more conscious of the way the dress-made-for-dancing reveals more than it should. I am glad for the elegance of high heels, the seduction of perfume as I walk towards him. Bold in the face of their timidity, wearing the passions that they hide. He is grateful for my casual presence as he stands to a side, uncomfortable with a dynamic we both understand. I have merely mentioned the music, not asked him to dance, and yet he gulps the cheap, bad alcohol and takes my hand. His arms are tight around my waist, its narrowness my pleasure as much as it is his, his hold a clinging as much as it is a taking. I listen to the wine-warmed words against my hair, love, love! Suddenly *love*! The sensation of a mouth half hidden. We are the center. Black prose on a bleached page. Beautiful. And when he mentions the noise, the need for fresh air, I go. Walking away beside the one they desire, I take the light with me. I take the rhythm, I take the music, I take the night. I take him from them because I can.

φ

CARELESS FISH
Nicole Louise Reid

THERE WAS A BOY, ONCE, who dove into our lake. I didn't know him. No one did. It was years before we ever moved here. Still, he is a boy. He dove from shore, like we all know not to do, and careened into a sunken trashcan lying on its side. The board of directors still pays the lawyers and he still is a stuck boy—smashed and limp, I imagine, in his chair or bed.

Lake water is green with all the algae my father says means it's healthy. Slimy, tangly, tickly. There's no way to see bottom beyond the first foot from shore. There may be sunken cans everywhere. In the two weeks of enough cold—end of January and beginning February— the water freezes silver and grey: every ripple of water reluctant to freeze, every layer paints the walls of hundreds of trashcans. In winter, I swear never to swim again. In winter, I tell my brother he's never to dive again. He doesn't listen. He loves the row of thick pilings along the inlet wall. All summer, he climbs them, then stands straight as they do, and in one breath he's in the air, a fairy tern finding krill. I watch his splash, smaller, smaller, until I can't stand it anymore. Until I'm sure he's lying smashed on the silty floor. But then finally is his surface explosion for air.

The lake's board now chains its cans to willow trees along the beach. But I haven't any confidence they dredged them all. My uncle has a metal detector for coins and bits of other people's jewelry. Sometimes I think I'll sneak it out of his shed, run the weed-whacker end over the lake's green water. But the shed is padlocked and I haven't a clue where he keeps the key. Anyhow, this is not the way they found so many old battered cans sunken deep in the muck. They sent teenaged boys with snorkels and masks and flippers to skim the lakebed, their hands stretched a full foot before them feeling for the large, metal things. Each time they sent out a boy, he came back with a can tethered to his ankle—drug down from the waist, only his snorkel and arms and sometimes his mask broke surface. And each time they sent out another boy, he came back with a trashcan, too. But everyone went home when the last boy came back buoyant. I knew this boy. He was the one in sixth grade who stood in the back of the bus for the sake of being the one standing, who made Ds on handwriting because his fist tightened so when he wrote cursive that his desk sometimes shook leg to wobbly leg, and who named the squirrels in his yard and took copious notes as to where each one buried a nut. As far as we were concerned back then and still now, *he* was the nut. It is with total certainty that I know he left the rest of the cans down there, maybe to map in a wicked scrawl on the pages of his notepad.

Dad brings home papers from the board, about the boy and the can and how much money he wants. "It'd be cheaper if he'd died," he says. "Cheaper and quicker if I'd shot him myself. Dumbass kid. Not even a member."

"Everyone knows not to dive," I say. "He *was* diving, wasn't he?"

"Survival of the fittest," says my brother because he thinks anyone good at anything can do it no matter the circumstance.

Dad nods, drops a brown-sauced broccoli down the front of his shirt. "Dammit to hell," he says.

"But the can," I say. "The water's too dark."

He picks up Chinese food some nights, when Mother—who hates it—is out and he's tired of me complaining about the tomato guck all over the chicken, or olives hiding in the taco meat. We're all getting older. I'm in love with a boy who kisses me, who tells me things—one who says he knew me in junior high. He's tall, years older, is a senior at another high school, plays drums in a band, and never lies. These are the things I love about him. The rest, I don't see.

After beef with broccoli and kung pao chicken—I save a pile of cashews for Mother—my brother shuts himself back into his basement room. No one in the house knows what goes on in there, but for me it's a land of particular intrigue. Posters and magazines, and I creep in there whenever I'm rattling around the house alone, to know what boys like.

The boy I love shows up at the downstairs door and we're walking down the driveway heading across the road to the beach, both knowing what will go on there. The wide, rock drive in through the trees is always worse than I remember, and I'm only wearing flimsy flats.

I should say here that I am a big girl. Almost sixteen years old and wearing a size 22. (I am just about to stop eating and drop to a size 10.But I'll be back up in the twenties soon, and even bigger.)I'm wearing a loose men's shirt pulled out over my shorts. I am smart and tender, and I believe that will help.

The boy has my hand and he's nervous, pushy. He's walking faster than I want to over these rocks that push up jagged edges into my arches and split the skin between my toes. First we sit in the sand. I'm never sure how it happens, something distracts me—a breeze dancing the willow whips, an owl high in the pines backing the row of houses that rims this inlet, a breath—and he's on me. In a lovely way. In a way I only remember as happening then. Before I knew to climb on, too. When all that happened did so because *he* wanted it. The purity in singly-intended moments is such a comfort.

There is a moon tonight so silvery-wide I squint. I'm not thinking about the sand in my shorts, in my waistband, in my hair. What I'm thinking is that I am a walrus, a sea lion, a thigmotactic beast and I never knew how much I needed to be touched before this night.

He pushes and I squirm. He can hardly breathe and every breath I let go is heat. Only a few months later I'll figure out this rolling, this stifled want, is worlds better than sex; but then it will be too late, a boy won't go back and a girl like me won't ask.

When he can't stand it any longer, the way I rub beneath him but keep his hand from unbuttoning his jeans, he rolls off of me and sits up hunched over his knees. Sometimes, when we're in the car, he'll get out, walk away from me, around the corner of a building and stand there like he's peeing. I'm not supposed to watch, but there are times I see his arm yanking like to unstick his zipper.

I loop my fingers in his waistband, tug at his back. "Soon," I say.

I've been saying this the two weeks we've been driving into the backs of strip malls, or coming to the lake at night. He just breathes real deep and then lets it all out in one big push of hating me. I remember to thank the stars he always lets me know where I stand with him, then feel a little sick brushing off the sand from my belly and thighs, the small of my back, too. The insides of my legs are raw with his denim. I rub at them, hold my skin in a silly little apology to myself. At a party within the year, I'll go into a master bath to wash myself like this, knowing that boy's already gone.

The coming apart. That is what I hate now, and what I will always hate.

I walk the peninsula of goose-pooped grass, see the deck houses — some lit, some dark — who've figured it out, the way to keep someone near. I push through woody forsythia and honeysuckle to find the turtles' log. It's maybe seven feet long, wide, smooth as rock, a tree limb along the marshy shore here. I step onto it. I step again, step until I'm near middle. The boy is watching from up on the beach, smiling, wondering. And I'm wondering, too. About who I am and how he found me. Counting myself lucky again. Any question why isn't in me yet, won't be until he's gone and I think things are clearer.

"Don't fall!" he calls out over the water, more an invitation than a warning.

I take another step. The lake surface is black with only half-shimmers of moon like careless fish sleeping on the water. From here I can see the chimney of my house up on its hill. I can see both our tulip poplars though not the oaks. I take another step.

"You going swimming?" he says, still watching me, still laughing.

I smile, push bangs aside and a bit of hair over my ear. I've never been this far out in the water swimming. I may have let a finger slip in from over the edge of our canoe. But where I am on this log jutting out of the lake wall, this is where the snakes burrow, where the water is deep enough for both diving and trashcans. I'm feeling reckless: with every step, a little voice says *slip* or *jump in*. It's enough to catch the energy in my feet, in my legs, but soft enough to keep me standing steady.

There are practicalities, too. Of clothing and hair. Of nakedness and moonlight. In a new moon, maybe I'd pretend he couldn't see me. But only a sliver bitten out of the night is too much light. Maybe.

Now I walk the log like a balance beam, remind myself I was a ballerina for eight years. First I merely point my toes, turn out my feet, slip them out in, out in. An arabesque. *Petits jetés* and *grands jetés*. I am showing off and it's silly. *Glissade, rond de jambe.* A sort of performance for him: I was someone way before you met me, I mean to holler but don't know what it is yet that makes me feel small.

I don't fall in the water. I could, if that voice were louder. What I do is slip out of my shorts, my shirt. Fashion a *pas de bourrée* along this log. And then I step into the lake, deeper at first than I'd even expected. I stumble some feeling the slime come up over my toes, then catch my footing. I move one bit farther and there is no floor beneath me, just the brushing of plant and fish against my legs—they're sniffing me, like my brother always says they do before they bite. I shift onto my back, float an awkward bent-at-the-middle float of girls not wanting water in their ears or for the heap of their bellies to show. But I relax, push flat my middle, feel the lapping in and over my ears, in and over, in and over. I slowly spin because the water moves me and the breeze helps, too. I must appear a wet-footed mosquito twirling across the surface.

I experience this night like a dream. Something I'm creating and something I will want to remember when I wake. Each thing that happens, I run it through my head, record it for morning.

He calls to me. My name. Such a wonderful thing, a name in a boy's mouth. The sound shouted over water comes in through the shifting of wet holding me up. I don't change a thing because I am spinning and this is what the boys want, right? It drives them wild to want.

"Come on," he's saying. His voice is different now; he's standing, moving around on the beach. "Get out of the water. Come on." It doesn't occur to me that he sees what I am, what he can have (and can't).

I am moving with the water, farther into the lake, almost out of the inlet that comes to our tiny shore.

"It's late!" he's calling.

Floating in this night with its moon and its breeze, I know—if I'm honest—that he saw me on the log, half-naked with gravity, and was startled by where the flesh swells. And with my eyes used to the stars, I know he holds my hand and sucks at my ears because he hopes he won't have to roll off of me later. He wants the word yes and my shorts and undies folded in the willow whips beside us.

What I want is for him to dive from the first piling, the most shallow-footed piling, into water just deep enough to sit beneath, just deep enough to never see it coming—the silty bottom and silver can smashed and bent from that first boy who dove into the shallows.

"This is stupid!" he shouts. "I'm not gonna wait!"

He leaves. I hear him on the rocks already: the gritty shifting of edges to edges under him. I hear the Volvo start at the bottom of my hill. I hear the engine close and then gone.

A minute of panic when I notice how far out I've drifted into the open water, the water that pushes off every which way to the separate inlets and beaches. I'm not certain which is ours until I see my white denim shorts in the bush. Then I float to shore, kicking some to make it faster. I see nothing but moon and shaggy branches of the sweetgums over me. I reach land and I'm freezing. Slivers of me feel missing like I am the moon and tonight is not my night for being whole.

I find my shoes, walk the grass for my shorts and shirt. He is gone. I made that happen.

I wring my hair, dotting the sand wet in dribbly dots. I dress and walk the rocks, barefoot this time. Something about this night needs to be felt, so I let my feet take it; the rest I lose along the path. I walk our steep drive, go in the downstairs door, see my brother's door open, the light off. He's on the stairs, stops a second to look at me drenched and shivering: "What happened to you?"

I shake my head 'cause I don't know.

He lifts his eyebrows and shrugs like I'm the one withholding information, and heads upstairs.

This is dangerous, but I go in. I kneel before his bookshelf, pull out magazine after magazine: *Playboy, Penthouse, Hustler, Oui.* I look at anything print. But they don't understand it any more than I do. They're way past the moment of decision. They don't mind because no one's rolling off in these magazines. No one's minding the moonlight or the fingers slipped up a shorts leg. No one's being left spinning in a lake. No one's choosing the water over him.

There are secrets in here. But I don't know the language yet, of legs spread and fingers slipped inside their mouths, of the differences between them and me standing on the turtles' log in a bright moon, of what I should want, what I'm expected to want.

He was never holding my hand. He was shaking it, trying to close the deal.

Once he took me to a suspension bridge over a little river. We lay down on it and he said he loved me. But he said things like that weren't stable; they were always changing. "For now," he said, "right now I love you." And I remember thinking I'd work to hold on to that. That afternoon, the sun fell pink and purple, and the orange was in his hair. There was no breeze and so as we lay on our backs, our feet at opposite ends, our heads side by side, while I grinned and wondered what I'd done to be so lucky, he gripped a rope and pushed his body in the other direction half-dumping me into the water to begin us swinging side to side. I knew right then, if I'm honest, that his moment had passed.

Tonight I slip the magazines back into place along my brother's shelf. I go on to my room and am not caught leaving his. I curl in to bed, a soggy mess of tangled hair and sandy feet, of wet underwear clinging to me. But there are some things one shouldn't have to look at, and so I stay clothed all night. This is the night I stop eating. Not for the reasons my father drinks scoopfuls of vanilla Slim-Fast in milk twice a day. I stop eating because there seems no other way, to be touched, to be held some nights, to be careless.

φ

THE LAST TIME
Herta B. Feely

THE LAST TIME I SAW HIM, in 1975, he walked through the door of the small Berkeley house I shared with two women, and my girlfriend's Doberman bit him in the knee. I thought he deserved that—at least that. He deserved worse. I also thought dogs know who's good and who's bad. They bite the bad ones.

The time before that, maybe early 1974, I saw him in his San Francisco flat, and he started screaming and hitting me, blaming me for things I hadn't done. Then he ran to the back of his apartment and I thought he was getting a gun, so I ran outside slamming the door behind me. It opened a moment later, and I thought he might shoot me in the back, but he only threw my suitcase at me.

Collecting my leather bag had been the pretext for my visit; the real reason had been to see him—one last time, I told myself—because, after all, I'd spent three months in a Colombian prison and weeks had passed since I'd returned and he'd refused to see me.

I was desperate to talk to him to find out what had happened after I last saw him leaving the customs area at the Bogotá airport. Of the four of us, he was the only one not carrying—the brains behind the operation never carries. I also hoped he might finally show a little sympathy or appreciation for my time in Buen Pastor. He hadn't sent a single note, though he had sent money. At the time, in 1973, I convinced myself that this alone meant he still cared. I clung to that belief through each endless day of waiting, through each promise that I'd be released and wasn't.

I don't remember much about the last time I saw him, except the surprise that registered on his face when the dog chomped on his knee, the sense of injustice, the pain. He was tall, lean, and handsome. But that day he looked disheveled, disoriented, not like the guy who'd wooed me and who I'd fallen for two years earlier.

A few months after the last time, I heard the police had found his body dumped somewhere along Highway 1 outside San Francisco.

He'd died of an overdose of heroin. Though he deserved the dog bite, he didn't deserve to die like that.

The last time I saw him was in a dream not long ago. He was smiling, easygoing, elusive, just as he'd been in life. I was drawn to him as we spoke. When the time arrived for yet one more separation, he told me to call him. Part of me wanted to, and yet this time I knew I wouldn't.

φ

DESIRE
Elly Williams

IN AUGUST, 1990, I MET HIM—let's call him Greg—at Bread Loaf. The Writers' Conference. It should suffice for you to know that this is a place nestled in Vermont's Green Mountains where lots of illicit sex takes place, affairs drenched in booze. Kisses laced with liquor and lies. Lauren Slater writes about it in her book *Lying: An Autobiographical Memoir.* She's seventeen and has wangled her way into the conference. A famous well-published writer—one of the faculty—seduces her—body and mind. This invasion goes on for two or more years. But, of course, she could be lying.

I'm not lying. This is truth.

Me—well—I was thirty-eight years old, married with two kids. I wasn't seventeen and taken in by a smarmy old man. No, I ensnared a man one year older than I, a divorced guy, an unpublished poet, who wasn't happy about me being married at all. But it didn't happen all that fast, not really. And while I did set about getting him interested in me, I didn't want to get involved; I just couldn't seem to stop myself, and I had no idea why. I had attended numerous writing conferences and always managed to carry on an emotional romance filled with whispery "I love you's" and "If only's." No sex. Not the actual act. Necking. Slick tongues. Eager hands. And a heart and body that came alive. I always returned home feeling like a tramp, but I could not stop myself. I did the same thing in whatever school at which I taught. Never did it occur to me that perhaps something was lacking in my marriage.

I had actually gone to the Bread Loaf Writers' Conference in 1990 with two goals: one, to have my manuscript chosen to be workshopped (it was—by Andrea Barrett, no less) and two, not to start up a flirtation. I needed to prove to myself I was not a slut.

But I was.

Here's the deal. Here's how it was with me for years and years. All the way back to junior high school. The rules changed over the years, but I played the same game. A game that I never understood. A game that hurt others and left me feeling either like nothing or like a slut. In high school the rules were: *Get a guy interested. Make out. Don't have sex.* Not in those days. Only bad girls had sex. I didn't even take off my clothes. I went to local parking spots like the dirt road on South Mountain or the evergreen-choked hills above Ross Park and necked for hours. I picked guys that I somehow sensed would fall in love with me, and they did. Gene. Rick. Frankie. Dan. Bill. Donnie. Craig. Oh, the wonder of an adolescent boy's panting desire and tentative gentleness was glorious. I loved the smell of them. Each one smelled differently. Gene had a faint odor of sweat, not unpleasant, kind of like car oil. Bill smelled of corn. I don't know why. We lived in the city. Craig smelled of rich warm coffee. Rick emanated a damp, hot overwhelming heat, chlorine from his swim team practices streaking through the heat making him a hot, wet pool of boy. When he wrapped me in his arms, lips tight against my neck or glued to my mouth, our tongues making us one—a hand slipping toward a breast, a thigh, how I loved it. The car windows sweating just as we were. Cloudy with unfulfillment. But as soon as those boys whispered, "I love you," it was over. The guy banished. With the snap of a finger and thumb, a blink of an eye. I didn't even tell them. They had to figure it out for themselves.

I felt nothing. At best I would say I felt a mini-black death of something inside me. When or if the guy chased after me, trying to understand what he'd done wrong, I refused to speak to him. What could I say? I had no understanding of my behavior. Looking back, maybe I felt pleasure at hurting some boy. Maybe for the second or two it took him to say I love you, I felt loved. But once the words floated from his mouth to the air they drizzled into a foggy nothingness. A goo worse than lies. An abyss.

A startling new memory: *My mother thought it was funny. Yes, she enjoyed my treatment of the boyfriends. I think she saw it as her revenge against men. But one time she's not laughing at all. She's very angry with me. I am a senior in high school. Binghamton Central High School in the Southern Tier of New York state, a state where my mother's father, my beloved grandfather Bah, was Chancellor of the Board of Regents and also responsible for bringing SUNY Binghamton to Binghamton. I have been dating my beloved older brother John's college fraternity buddy, Paul. John and I are close. John is only a year older than I, and he has always liked to* *monitor my love life. So this is perfect. I take the bus from Binghamton to Clinton, New York, where John and Paul go to Hamilton College. John is the seventh generation of my family to attend Hamilton. My prom comes in the middle of the year—in late December because at that time you could start school in September or January depending on your birthday. I had a September birthday but had skipped half of third grade—thus giving me a December graduation. So Paul is my date. Instead of going out to eat, we set up a cozy dining room in a corner of our Binghamton house's basement. Charlie and Cari, my younger brother and sister, are both waiters and spies. Charlie is two years younger than I, Cari eight. They are to listen to what we say to each other in the flickering candlelight and repeat our words to my mother. Paul leans across the table in his dark suit and striped tie, all ready for the prom. "I love you," he says. My white tulle gown, which would be worn for my coming-out party the next year, crumples as I move closer to him and say, "I love you, too," not having the faintest idea what it would mean to love someone. I break up with him that night at the prom. He has no idea what hit him or why. I don't know, either. Emptiness. That's what I feel.*

Here's where my mother acts out of character. She's furious with me for breaking up with Paul. It's not funny to her at all. She is so angry that she doesn't attend my high school graduation (nor does my father—his excuse being he's working), and she doesn't speak to me for at least two weeks.

I don't get it.

A year or two earlier I dated a boy—Darrell Darrow—in Hallstead, Pennsylvania, where our second home is. It's a farm located on 1,000 acres lost in Pennsylvania's Endless Mountains. Darrell was a nice boy as was Paul, and we would talk of marriage. My mother prodded me forward with these plans. Why? I was sixteen years old.

I didn't just break up with boys who told me they love me.

Worse.

I had a double life with boys. I set up scenarios where there was the good boyfriend—the one who didn't press me for a bare-tit feel or a hand in my pants or for me to suck him—and then there was the bad boyfriend. He was the one to whom I was attracted, and we'd wrestle and dry-hump and tongue kiss until we were both sore. I see now that this double life, this constant two-timing was an imprint—something that my soul carried within it for as long as I could remember. Ah, that is an interesting word. **Remember.** If you remember something does that make it true? Are my memories more true than false? I don't know these answers, but I know it was easy to carry on my double life with boyfriends because my family had two homes and two completely separate lives depending which home we were living in at the time. But I don't know why I led a double life with boyfriends—I couldn't stop myself. It was as if such behavior had been imprinted on me at birth.

I think it is important that you understand exactly what is meant by imprint.

I learned about imprinting in junior high school in Mrs. Barnes's science class while sitting next to Frankie Hanks on whom I had a crush. He took care of all the frog dissection. Mrs. Barnes told us that the imprinting ability is one of the strongest forces in nature, the strongest in geese. Ducks come in second. No one understands exactly what happens inside a gosling's brain, but the results are unmistakable: A gosling knows it is the same species as whatever living creature larger than itself it sees upon hatching or shortly thereafter. It doesn't think it is, it doesn't use the creature for a replacement until it finds its own species, it doesn't pretend to be that species; it is that species in its mind.

A fact: *Suicide runs in families. For instance, Spaulding Gray's mother killed herself when he was a child. Depression plagued him all his life. He suffered the seduction of suicide — the trauma of a parent's suicide reflected mirror-like in the fate of the child. Slated for suicide. And why not? Your parent doesn't love you enough to stay alive for you, that sensuous seduction of a fate **imprinted** on you is too powerful. You know Gray jumped from the Staten Island Ferry to his death, don't you, **leaving behind two sons?** No accident, that. John Berryman's father committed suicide. John Berryman jumped to his death off the Washington Avenue Bridge in Minneapolis. Hunter S. Thompson shot himself to death. Gunshot wound to the head. **His son found the body.** When Conrad Aiken, the poet, novelist, and short story writer was twelve, he saw his father kill his mother, then shoot himself. The rest of his life he believed he was fated for suicide. He suffered debilitating depressions. That feeling informed all his writings. Have you read his "Silent Snow, Secret Snow?" You might want to. It's about a twelve year old boy who decides to retreat behind a wall of drifting snow to escape life, to fall into schizophrenia as a way out of pain. Suicide's power obliquely or directly affects much of a writer's work.*

I wondered if being a slut had been imprinted on me at birth. I didn't see how. My mother wasn't a slut as far as I knew, and my father worked all the time as an ob-gyn in two different hospitals: Binghamton General and Our Lady of Lourdes. Chief of Staff there. Later, he worked in several other nearby hospitals, and I know he practiced near our farm in Montrose, Pennsylvania for a while, too. How could I be an imprinted slut? I didn't know.

What I do know is that when I did get married, I married someone I didn't love and wasn't sexually attracted to— he didn't fall into either category—the good boy or the bad boy. I know he had a wild side just as I did, and I know he was handsome. I know that before I dated him, I had been desperately in love with a man named Zach Moore. I would have married him in heartbeat. His name alone turned me to a wiggly, jiggly ooze of Jell-O. Cherry flavored. It was September 1970. At the time I was a freshman at Hood, then an all-girls college, in Frederick, MD—the same school my mother had attended. Zach was good and bad. Whenever we went parking, we drove to the forbidden caves, the caverns above the old Shookstown Road haunted by a local monster called the Dwayo. The caves are silent, otherworldly silent, not even the sound of trickling water breaks the stillness. They are filled with the hush of fear. We stepped inside a cave and spread out a blanket, the dread of the ghostly Dwayo and the luscious fear of going all the way tangling inside me. It's like drinking stolen beer, the liquor burning my throat, mixed with Zach's rubbing his cheek, its slight stubble deliciously rough against my skin and smelling vaguely of cologne. Oh, how I loved those burning sensations, the faint tingle of a man's skin mixed with the odor of what? Old Spice? Bay Rum? Oh, yes. Tantalizing.

I never once two-timed him—unless you count my seeing one of my old high-school boyfriends during Christmas break.

Okay, so I did cheat on him—but Zach and I weren't having sex and Ben, my last high-school boyfriend, and I weren't either. We necked and dry humped until our skin was raw.

Neither Ben nor Zach ever said, "I love you." Both broke up with me. I met my husband—R—I can't bear to say his name—on the rebound. It was now February 1971 and I was still a freshman at Hood. I was hanging out in Smith Hall's waiting room—those were the days of parietals and girl guests being announced over the intercom as visitors and boy guests being announced as callers. A secret code. I was down in that waiting room hoping Zach would show up. R was hanging around hoping Sharon Ayers would show up. Neither one did.

Estella, the desk girl, a scholarship student who sat at the desk to earn money—we Hood girls all knew who the scholarship students were—they were the ones who sat behind the dorm desks or waited on the linen-draped tables at which the rest of us dined. Anyway, Estella, introduced us. R invited me out for a beer—he was old enough to buy—he was twenty-two years to my eighteen —and we climbed into his parents' wreck of a drab olive-green Rambler station wagon, stopped at a nearby liquor store for a six-pack, and R headed straight for Poole Jones Road, a dirt road on the outskirts of town. He took off his glasses and lunged at me. I wasn't afraid, though. We kissed a little, but mostly talked. It turned out he was a Frederick townie, and he'd dropped out of the University of Maryland and was living at home, delivering Dairy Maid Milk to earn money. He had to make the payments on his Opal Cadet. He delivered milk to President Nixon at Camp David.Something about him felt familiar. As if I had known him all my life. It wasn't his smell—stale meatloaf, a little congealed gravy, almost musky. I don't mean the sensual musk of some perfumes or that all encompassing juicy odor from having sex. I mean I imagined the smell of the musk deer that Mrs. Barnes taught us about in science class. The male musk deer lacks antlers but possesses long canine teeth and secretes musk from an abdominal gland. No fresh corn, chlorine or cologne here. Maybe it was milk gone bad. Within four months I had sex with him. With my clothes off. Sex. Penis inside vagina. The fact of having it is what was exciting. Illicit. I called up my best friend and said, "Does my voice sound any different?" She didn't know what I was talking about. But I was pleased with myself.

I knew that if I had sex before I got married—forbidden fruit—I would burn in hell. I got that from attending the Episcopal Church for seventeen years. This knowledge also came from a father who arrived home from the hospital or office and told his family at the dinner table stories from his day. Once he told us about a headless baby he'd delivered. Another time he told us about an armless, legless baby. We heard about the double genitalia babies, too. And fat women. His nurses couldn't weigh them on the office scales. They had to go to the railroad depot to be weighed. I don't know if that's true. I never thought about it until right now as I sit at my desk writing this memoir. What is memory? What is the past? What is this past of mine that so informs my present? How real is it? Am I a revisionist? Did he really tell us these stories? Do fat people really have to be weighed at railroad depots? I remember — or should I say I think I remember — ah — there's that word again — REMEMBER — that his favorite topic was pregnant, unwed girls. Sluts. His face would turn red and shiny, a vein pop from his forehead. Sluts, he'd say, spittle forming at the corners of his mouth.

So you must realize that implicit in R's and my illicit sex act was the awareness that we would get married. No way out. Ever. Divorce was far worse than fat women or pregnant, unwed girls. It was unspeakable.

Something you should know: *By the time R and I had been going out three or four months, he'd already bloodied my lip, bruised my cheekbones, and beaten his mother badly. He had a huge poster of me hanging in his room and he and a friend took a roll of toilet paper and hung it over the picture so that the toilet paper covered my face. Even this didn't make me think I should break up with him. Why should I? I was worthless. Someone who had premarital sex. A slut. Something I'd somehow known all along.*

Something else you should know: *By fall of my sophomore year at Hood, I knew I didn't like having sex with R. It was something I did as infrequently as possible, taking off as few clothes as I could. I just wanted it over with. I'd count or think about homework or what clothes to wear for dinner when my grandparents visited, anything that took me away from the reality of what was happening to me. I thought that was what sex was like for everybody.*

I married R halfway through my senior year in college.

*

Bread Loaf. August 1990. Total proof of slutdom. I fail hopelessly in my goal not to carry on a flirtation. The flirtation swirls out of control. My feelings actually engage with a man for the first time in my life because Greg reciprocates them. We do not have sex. I am married, after all, but I know now that after seventeen years of a dead marriage, I am going home, and I am going to ask for a divorce. This will be the third time I ask for a divorce. Only this time I will carry out my desire. Funny word choice for a divorce, isn't it? DESIRE.

φ

THE GRASS WIDOW
A. Terrell Washington

I AM A GRASS WIDOW — you know, an abandoned mistress. My lover finally departed with the first round of last spring's roses. I felt like the lawn getting a fresh cut, the first of the growing season, which every landscaper knows is as painful for the lawn as it is for the lawnmower. Though grieving, I spread grass seed, forcing the spotty brown lawn to become a lush green carpet. Now, I love nothing better than to dig deep in the dirt. I'm happiest when I am smelly and sweaty and covered in potting soil.

At my doctor's prescription a few years ago, I took up gardening to "calm down" and lower my blood pressure after a trial-run breakup. I purchased hot-house flowers in decorative clay pots which I placed in pretty places along the cracked cement patio. Of course, they perished posthaste. By the third season, my lover had vanished too, but my children presented me with a potter's bench for my birthday. So, I picked up a spade and a shovel and started planting daffodil bulbs and marigold seedlings to bury him and my heart in what Cousin Maurice christened "The Secret Garden of Eden" —the transformed space that used to be my barren backyard.

A "grass widow," according to *Webster's,* is a woman whose husband is temporarily absent by divorce or separation, the mother of a child born out of wedlock, or an abandoned mistress.

I fit into the latter definition, though I preferred to think of myself as the sanctioned soul mate, the second wife, of the husband of my heart. A woman of independent means, I was not your stereotypical *cortegiana honesta,* elevated to the royal status of the 16th century Venetian poetess Verona Franco, who was immortalized in the book *The Honest Courtesan* and the film *Dangerous Beauty.* More of an exalted concubine in the early Biblical tradition, I was no Flavor-of-the-Month Floozy either.

The 16th century origin of a "grace widow" implies "a widow by courtesy" or "one who becomes a widow by grace or favour, not of necessity, as by death." So, I prayed that by the "grace" of God, *viducca de gratia*, more aptly applied to me.

According to Dictionary.com, the antiquated moniker is "perhaps an allusion to a bed of grass or hay as opposed to a real bed." Later, "after the sense of 'grass' had been obscured, people may have interpreted 'grass' as equivalent to the figurative use of 'pasture,' as in 'out to pasture'." According to bootlegbooks.com, "during the gold mania in California a man would not infrequently put his wife and children to board with some family while he went to the 'diggings.' This he called 'putting his wife to grass,' as we put a horse to grass when not wanted or unfit for work."

In a more contemporary context, "grass widow" refers to a woman whose husband is away for a while either physically or emotionally.

For all intents and purposes, I was a mistress who built a loving life with a heart-husband whose physical presence was unpredictable. Suddenly, a near-death experience sliced me from his trunk like a pruned twig and thrust me into wicked grass widowhood. Ironically, he was stung by a bee while plowing a pasture and he awoke in an emergency room where he had been hastily revived from anaphylactic shock. His limbs broke and his tendons tore in a near fatal fall and he was laid up in his vineyard asylum in the Blue Ridge foothills for what seemed an eternity. He believed he was about to meet his Maker. I believed he bumped his brain, hemorrhaged his heart and severed his soul. In hindsight, I remember I dreamed that he died that day, and he languished long enough to stumble a forewarning: "I almost did." Sure enough, my dream became my waking death. For his temporary injury turned into a permanent disability and a strange—and estranged—bird emerged, one who never flew into the lovers' nest in our Secret Garden of Eden again.

There are all manner of marriages and all manner of ways to grieve their inevitable dissolution. Even in the best of unions, C.S. Lewis in "A Grief Observed," says that each partner understands that one day one of them will die or depart and leave the other a widow or widower. Somehow, you must survive the loss of love.

*

Gardener of my Soil and Soul

So, to survive the loss of love, I became an obsessed gardener. I transformed my abandoned bed of hay into a bolstering bed of begonias. Not naturally an early riser, I took to getting up at the crack of dawn to see what surprises my secret garden grew. As a novice, I didn't know a fundamental fact about watering and pampering and fertilizing flowers, or pruning prickly twigs. I bought a copy of "Gardening for Dummies" to learn the difference between perennials and annuals. I believed my love was a perennial because he kept coming back. He turned out to be the latter like the Easter lily that failed to reappear that same year. Gardening, I discovered that cutting the dead petunia petals from their stems and the dead weight from my life produced joy, fullness of self, and fruit from the vine.

I became the gardener of my soul as well as the gardener of my soil. In Bruce Wilkinson's *Secrets of the Vine: Breaking through to Abundance*, he writes that "He is the vine and we are the branches." The Holy Spirit transforms you so you become even more useful and "bear much fruit" for His glory. Watering became my meditation; digging became my prayer and pruning my discipline. No longer self-absorbed, my blood pressure reading returned to normal—from 130/90 to 110/80. No longer a novice, I grew fruit in my garden as well as flowers.

Wilkinson's parable advises: "If your life bears no fruit, God will intervene to discipline you. If your life bears some fruit, God will intervene to prune you. If your life bears a lot of fruit, God will invite you to abide more deeply with Him." Discipline removes sin. Pruning changes priorities. Abiding requires acting according to His will to do the work we are called to do to make a better world, create a more abundant harvest.

Or, as the R&B band "Earth, Wind and Fire" sang: "If there ain't no beauty, you got to make some beauty; have mercy." Thus, a grapevine grows along my stockade fence. Tomatoes overtake the potted plants. No matter where you sit, you're treated to ornamental accoutrements that adorn my bountiful backyard garden. Hidden in the leaves and vines are curios I crafted out of my grief. Prominently displayed are the garden gifts presented from my family, my friends and even my lost lover, for whom I hung a Cape Hatteras hammock in a cool corner between two ivy-covered oak trees.

*

Winter Weary Heart and Hands

Months later, the snowflakes are prancing outside my picture window. I flick the butane lighter to set ablaze the paper log. The instantly glowing fireplace sets a wintry stage, accompanied by Miles Davis' "Kind of Blue" as the soundtrack. Around me I wrap the king-sized afghan, the colorful cozy keepsake my godmother, "Queenie," crocheted for me before she died.

As I warm my hands on my favorite mug filled with Cuban coffee, Kahlua and hazelnut cream, a sudden draft shakes me to shivers. I feel the chill seep deep into my chest. I know instinctively that it is not winter's blast that causes the cold. My unshakable grief is the cold-hearted culprit. I miss my Mommas. I miss my Aunties. Most of all, I miss my man.

At this snowy season, the abandoned hammock is rolled up and laid to rest in the drafty basement. The wrought iron birdbath is filled with frozen water. The trellised loveseat looks lonely. The collection of wind chimes makes a nerve-wracking noise. Snow blankets the azalea bushes. The lilies lie in wait.

Gazing on my icicle garden, I yearn to be caressed to fend off the deep freeze developing in my bones. I crave a body heat of precisely 98.6 degrees. I want to sizzle under my sunbonnet as I rip tomatoes from the vine. Instead, I must settle for self-sufficient substitutes and turn up the thermostat. Even as a child weathering blustery New Haven winters, I detested the housebound season. I suffer miserably from seasonal distress disorder. It doesn't help that I can't dig in the dirt, but I'm not about to shovel snow either.

My stocky, octogenarian neighbor, "Cap," for Captain, a military man who managed a bustling horticultural business for decades after retiring from the Army and still grows collard greens between our Southern suburban brick ramblers until the first frost, says he never met a woman who loved being outdoors as much as I do. Even he knows that joy rings true, as long as the thermometer doesn't dip below 40 degrees.

"Praise the Lord, if you had been a boy, you'd been a really good gardener," Cap offers as a compliment. Sarge rarely ends a sentence without acknowledging or thanking God.

Cap is a winter warrior. "What a blessing, I love it, this snow and cold weather, amen," he says. "It's so pretty, I just have to go out in it and touch it and open my mouth and let the snow drop in it."

Life's lessons come from dark clouds too, Cap preaches. "This (winter) weather's prosperous, good for the ground," says the human Farmer's Almanac dressed in a black and red plaid wool shirt, shovel in hand. "We'll have a glorious, green spring and better blossoms for it, yes Lordy."

Are these words of wisdom supposed to warm a "sho'nuff" winter weary heart? Is it spring yet? Please, I shout, not another snow day to grovel in my grief.

Hell, I must find something to do with my idle hands.

*

Oven Mitts for Garden Gloves

I reach for comfort. I reach for the spoon, the hand-me-down cracked, crooked wooden spoon. I know this spoon like I know my garden spade. I use it on the days I feel captive to the women—Mommie Bea, Gramma Della, Aunt Dovey, Aunt Minnie, and Aunt Lois—who have used it before me. This long-handled, scarred and scorched treasure has many bittersweet secrets of my foremothers to tell. And, I have gathered some skeletons in the cupboard to pass on to my daughter.

On this blustery day, I pull the spoon from the kitchen drawer that serves as a museum to my Aunties' cooking utensils and cutlery, and get busy to banish the blues. She baked a Gold Medal melt-in-your-mouth pound cake. In her honor, I cannot muster the mental or physical strength to stir by hand, as instructed, the pound of butter, half dozen eggs, milk, vanilla, three cups of sugar and four cups of double-sifted cake flour.

Still, I determine to exchange my gardening gloves for an oven mitt. After all, I do make a mean two-bean, ground turkey chili, sprinkled with grated cheese and served with garlic butter Texas Toast. I wake my daughter and teach her how to conjure up some spirited TLC (Tender Loving Care) with the adapted family recipe. I tweak the peppered pottage to taste like making hot-house, passionate love to my missing mate.

He loved the red, green, orange, and yellow peppers I pampered in the garden so much that for his 40th birthday, I purchased a vibrant shirt bursting with the spicy hot pods on a black background that became a water cooler conversation piece. His co-worker says everyone in their stuffy office sighs a happily relief when they take notice: "It must be spring because he's wearing that Chili Pepper shirt again." Naturally, I placed all manner of red and green pod-like accents and accessories around the kitchen and dubbed it the "Chili Pepper Palace," hoping to nourish us through the winter solstice. Last year, the hot house froze just as the spring planting season arrived.

*

Cultivating the Chili Pepper Palace

I don't cook. Well, not much, sometimes on Sundays to feed my grown children as a way of getting us in the same space at once. So, why did I become obsessed with cultivating the Chili Pepper Palace this winter? Why was I as pleased as punch when my new handyman finished installing the dishwasher that I dotted with red chili magnets to mark my labor of love's loss?

In *Around the House and in the Garden: A Memoir of Heartbreak, Healing and Home Improvement*, author Dominique Browning wrote after her divorce: "I cannot say my home healed my heart. But I can say that, as my heart healed, my home reflected it...We yearn to live in houses full of love, happiness, passion and peace, too. We yearn for domestic bliss. Even when we have found it, we are restless about wanting things to be better. As soon as we get what we want, we want more. That's the nature of being alive, of persevering, of striving. And that is the nature of redecorating."

A lifelong girlfriend reminds me that I've been talking about buying a dishwasher for ten years. I haven't had a dishwasher since I left my husband because he wouldn't leave me even after I demanded that he move. My legal spouse of twenty-five years wouldn't stop showing up at what he continued to call "his house," although I paid the mortgage for as long as either of us could remember.

I didn't want to leave my four-bedroom-three-bathroom, corner Colonial brick townhouse surrounded by tall trees and a block from the man-made lake. I didn't want to move back to the 1965 brick rambler, abutting an apartment complex, where I was raised and which I later inherited. I hated to part with my fully equipped kitchen with its gas range, refrigerator with an icemaker, stainless steel sink with a garbage disposal and especially my double-decker dishwasher. I hated to return to the dark kitchen of my youth with its burnt cabinets, chipped porcelain sink and rusting window. Oh, how I missed my marital home with its first floor wall of windows and the French door that led to the secluded flagstone patio that eventually cracked and crumbled like the chaotic couple who once basked in the sun there.

A decade later, as a happily divorced woman but a grieving grass widow, I set about redecorating the ravenous Chili Pepper Palace. The rubber gloves replaced the oven mitt. Bit-by-bit, like interlocking the joints of a super-sized jigsaw puzzle, I refreshed the kitchen scenery. I began by laying bright floor tiles to piece myself and my life back together. I feverishly scrubbed and bleached every visible surface from floor-to-ceiling, crawling on my hands and knees. "You're working it out, aren't you, Sistagirl," a friend asked at the scary site of me drenched in sweat and soap suds. I splurged on bright red table settings and striped, pepper-colored placemats. The UPS man struggled to deliver the heavy boxes containing a retro dining set I ordered from a catalog. The microwave oven, the sink, the garbage disposal, the icemaker and the ceiling fan were all replaced or repaired. Even the oak breadbox was exchanged for a newer metal model. A full view storm door and a garden window await Home Depot's back order.

Finally, a section of the painted white cabinets was cut to make room for the dishwasher. This top-of-the-line Sears Kenmore was fully equipped with bells and whistles, but I bought it for a steal of a deal one rebounding day I could afford to pay cash. By the time the dishwasher was whirling and whispering with its virgin load, I wondered, is my melancholy mission accomplished at last? Albeit alone, am I almost home and whole again? Am I just imagining that these dreary winter days are growing longer and lighter?

*

Grace from the Grieving Garden

"Houses and gardens express so much about ourselves, the state of our hearts, our lives," writes Browning in her memoir about "the way a house can express loss, and then bereavement, and then finally, the rebuilding of a life." She advises "there is no right time to begin again; the spirit has to move you…love does not stop; energy doesn't stand still; and neither do our houses," or our graceful gardens. "Gardening became my way of growing into the new life – digging in for the long haul, connecting, committing to a patch of soil, rooting in and under and round and through it all," Browning suggests. After all, "gardens are as much about the work that goes into them as they are about the results."

To patch the soil is to patch the pain.

Browning expresses gratitude for a beloved relative who kindled a passion for homemaking within her. She "gave me the tools of the *hausfrau* that would help me forge my way out of my grief."

But what consoling cog does a grass widow grip in the dead of winter when she longs to seek solace in the sleeping soil, which, in turn, longs for the tempting touch of her hardy hands? There are no Hallmark sympathy cards for grass widows. No warming caresses from a community of comforters. No therapeutic survivors' support group either. Your penance for living an unconventional life is to suffer its death in silence. My only outlet, my saving grace, is to burrow deep in the dirt. Cooking and cleaning are secondary substitutes.

For the moment, contentment contains this grass widow's challenge. The two-bean ground turkey chili is cooked and the Chili Pepper Palace is clean and cheery. Back in front of the fire, back under my Queenie blanket, I tuck my feet, snug in ski socks, under my buttocks and curl up in an overstuffed lounger. I sip a meaty Australian merlot and savor the heartwarming bowl of beans. I can feel my phantom lover, and my mourning is suspended. Soon enough this grass widow will gracefully and gratefully gaze again upon her grief garden, and see the crocuses arriving.

But it's not spring yet.

φ

THEY SHALL BE COMFORTED
Sandra Hunter

His daughter, Roxi, calls on Sunday evening. She makes an attempt at cheerful conversation— *It's a beautiful day here*—but then begins to cry. Arjun has difficulty understanding her, but finally makes out her words: "You're having the hospital bed delivered."

He realizes she has remembered what he said. *Once they put me in the hospital bed, it will be over.* That was a few months ago; perhaps he meant it at the time. Perhaps he never meant to get as far as the hospital bed.

He is no longer able to lie flat on his back; his breathing is difficult. The hospital bed will elevate him, although he hates seeing his knees pushed up like candlesticks.

Also, he can no longer get out of his bed unaided. He used to bring his knees up to his chest and kick to give him the impetus he needed to rolls out. But more often, now, it doesn't work. He can only kick twice and then he is helpless, lying half in, half out, waiting for someone to come and help him.

He does not want to go to hospital. He has told his wife and his son, Murad, who visits every other week. *Don't put me in hospital. Let me die at home.* He can never get through the second sentence before they crowd his words. *You're not going to die. You'll live a long while yet.* He is irritated with their inability to face death. After all, it's his death, not theirs. They shouldn't be so squeamish.

It isn't the hospital smell, the indifferent care of the hospital nurses, the barely concealed boredom of the doctors; it is the fact that he will not recognize anything there. He won't have his pictures of Rob, beloved four year-old grandson; the strange brown blob drawn by Rob and declared a teddy bear, the object made of sticks liberally smattered with glitter glue. No one knows what that one is. According to Rob, it's sometimes a windmill, sometimes a pirate's treasure box, a secret cave or garden.

Arjun would miss his back garden window. He can still reach it if he takes his time, carefully balancing his weight on his walker so that he won't suddenly tip backwards or sideways. He can stand there for a few minutes and gaze at the budding blue fir, or the overlong grass that Murad, his son, won't mow.

He sighs. Murad is a name anyone would be proud of. It is his own middle name and he passed it proudly to his son, who has now chosen to name himself Mike.

Arjun enjoys seeing this abundance of green life pushing up through the soil. He smiles at the wayward dandelions that raise their yellow-tufted heads. Sunila, his wife, will murder them later, carefully pouring on a solution that will turn them brown. The bright yellow heads remind him of his grandson's spiky black hair. He is secretly pleased that Roxi cannot comb or gel the renegade hair flat. Let Rob defy conventions; let him run wildly over the carefully kept garden, Sunila pursuing him and exhorting him not to stand on the new plants, Roxie in her fancy stiletto shoes, yelling pointless threats from the safety of the kitchen doorway.

Let Rob tear up the new lemon basil and bring handfuls back for his grandfather to smell. Meanwhile, Sunila and Roxi will complain and roll their eyes. Boys are so destructive.

But he will bury his nose into Rob's offering. *Smell, Grandpa.* And smile into the bright face. Yes, it smells wonderful. *Like lemon ice cream, Grandpa.* Yes, let's have some.

But they don't have ice cream. Sunila doesn't approve of ice cream and won't have it in the house. She claims she forgets, but he knows she hates ice cream. It makes her fat. So no one can have it. He secretly rejoices in her war against her weight. She is an old woman. Why should she care if she doesn't have an hourglass figure? Old women are for hugging, but Sunila hugs no one. She even hugs Rob carefully, not allowing more than his face to press to hers briefly, something Arjun will not forgive. He would give a good deal to hug his grandson.

The clear flute notes of Rob's voice opens everything, like a child's hinged dolls-house, as he pushes through the front door. Roxi follows in his wake, cautioning, hushing, attempting to suppress his bright voice.

"It's me, Grandpa." Rob crushes his head against Arjun's chest, then plants a soggy kiss on his cheek.

Arjun is joyful. "I'm so happy to see you, Rob."

Rob, ever hopeful, asks for ice cream. Sunila says, "Oh dear. I forgot to get some."

Rob looks at his grandfather.

"No ice cream, Grandpa?"

"Never mind, son, you can get some from the van when it comes by."

Sunila bustles into the conversation. "That van never comes here anymore. I don't know what happened to it."

Not even an hour later, the tinkling of "Greensleeves" announces the van and Sunila has to hide her disapproval and cough up the money for an ice cream cone.

"Get one with a chocolate flake, son."

"Okay, Grandpa." And he runs out as Roxi shouts about the traffic and runs behind him on precarious spiked heels.

Arjun mutters to himself. "She'll break her neck in those shoes."

Sunila says, "It's about time she bought something nice for herself. She never gets anything from that good-for-nothing man."

"They're divorced, Sunila."

"He should support her."

"She makes more money than he does."

Sunila sniffs and rubs her nose with the palm of her hand. He knows she is aware that he finds this dismissive gesture disgusting.

He cranes to see whether Rob has bought his ice cream. "Let him eat his ice cream in here."

"Not in here. There will be ice cream all over the place."

"What does it matter?"

"And who has to clean it up?"

There was a time when he would have had more energy over these disputes. He would have found a towel for the boy to sit on while he dripped ice cream happily over himself. But now he has no power, no choice, no freedom to say *But it is so*, with the finality that comes with a functioning body.

When the body no longer operates, the self disappears. He feels this diminishing, a gradual receding of who he is, what he likes, how he dresses, where he goes. And he can go nowhere. A short trip to the back window and he is tired enough to have to rest for a while on the sofa before he makes the trip back to the safety of his Laz-E-Boy.

He longs for the energy that would allow him to walk with his grandson by the seashore and go searching for treasure. *Let's dig for gold, Grandpa.* Do you have your shovel? Okay. Let's dig.

And he would slyly drop in a few polished pennies so that Rob can shout with delight, *Grandpa! Treasure!*

He longs for the flexibility that would make him able to stand, without assistance and reach up to one of the high shelves for a book that has pictures of elephants.

He looks around for Sunila, but she has gone into the kitchen to make tea, and instead, he asks Roxi, "Can you reach down the elephant book?"

Rob comes bouncing back in with his ice cream cone with a chocolate flake sticking proudly out, like a small flag. Arjun calls to him, holding the book open. "Look, Rob, see the tusks? This is a big guy."

"Did you have an elephant in India, Grandpa?"

"No, but I rode on one in Madras. And the elephants there are as tall as the ceiling."

"Are there lions?" Rob's eyes are huge.

"Tigers — huge tigers!"

"But the elephant is bigger than the tiger, isn't he Grandpa?"

"Oh, yes. And very brave and strong. The tiger won't attack the elephant. The elephant is the real king of the jungle."

He longs for musculature so that he can hold Rob's hand and give it a gentle squeeze, so that he can hold out his arms and receive his grandson for a hug, so that Rob can hug him back for there is nothing like a mutual hug. And he would hold out his arm for Rob to swing on, let Rob climb him like a tree.

But in the absence of these physical luxuries, he makes his voice as welcoming as possible. He tries to match Rob's enthusiasm with his own weaker echo.

Rob loses interest in the elephants and wanders around the living room.

Arjun stands carefully, allowing his body to find its balance before leaning forward onto the walker. Slowly, he edges himself to the sofa where he sinks onto a thick cushion.

Robs spins, jumps onto the sofa and thumps against his grandfather.

Arjun is overjoyed to be pummeled by his grandson, even though he feels himself losing his balance. A combination of fleeting reflex and a wild grab at the walker helps him remain upright.

"Is your ice cream delicious?"

"Here, Grandpa. You can have some."

The ice cream is thrust into his face and he opens his mouth to receive the gift. But the muscles don't respond properly. He can't bite and close his mouth around the ice cream, so it smears across his mouth and cheek. He is delighted to have tasted the ice cream, tasted what Rob can taste. Does he taste more than the cold sweetness, is there a richer chocolate taste in the young mouth?

Sunila comes in and begins fussing. "All over your face. You're a mess." She rubs at his face with a paper towel.

She puts her sweet, cajoling face on for Rob. "Let's go in the garden and eat your ice cream there."

His heart drops. There is nothing he can do. Even if he argues, she will win.

Rob says, "But what about Grandpa?"

"Grandpa's going to stay here while you finish your ice cream. Then you can come in and see him."

"But Grandpa wants ice cream, too."

Roxi says, "Go with Grandma, Rob."

Rob thrusts out the ice cream cone again, a last attempt to share, but feminine hands guide him away.

Sunila makes a joke. "You almost got Grandpa on the nose that time." She laughs.

He hears them in the kitchen, small exclamations of *Oh no*, and *Oops, let's get you outside quickly* as the women bundle the child into the garden. Sunila goes outside, too, and Roxi, he supposes, is leaning in the doorway. "Don't get ice cream on Grandma's roses, Rob."

He hears their voices from what sounds like a long way away. If he closes his eyes he will drift away. He is determined not to lose any of Rob's visit, so he levers himself up and inches the walker into the kitchen. At least he can stand by the window and watch.

Rob is walking in slow circles around the lawn, licking around the melting cone. He's eaten the flake. Arjun tries to imagine what it tastes like. He searches his mouth with his tongue for the memory of the brief taste, but it is gone.

Roxi and Sunila are standing together on the flagstones near the tiny greenhouse. They are probably discussing herbs and how coriander needs this and tomatoes need that. They don't know anything, the pair of them.

Arjun watches his grandson sit on a cement step. He puts his whole mouth over the cone and sucks. Arjun feels uneasy. What if he inhales the ice cream and chokes? He tries to lift his hand to the window to knock, to draw the chattering women's attention.

Rob yanks the ice cream out and drops it on the patio. He looks up at the window at Arjun, his mouth open in astonishment. His face turns red and he screams.

Arjun guesses a bee. He waves feebly at the women, but now they are fussing around the child, asking him questions. Rob screams, catching his breath in great swooping sobs.

Arjun finds he is breathing in great gusts, too. What if the boy swallows the sting? Rob will have to go to hospital, be put on a respirator. And what if he is allergic to bee stings?

He tries to knock on the window, but his hand cannot make a fist and his fingers scrape helplessly against the glass. Neither woman looks up; Rob's eyes are squeezed tight. Finally, more by luck than by rational deduction, Roxi darts her finger inside and extracts the sting.

He is relieved, his own mouth throbbing in sympathy. The two women manage to get the boy inside and suddenly the house is filled with his broken heart. An ice cream has bitten him. There is nothing left in the world.

The women are trying to console Rob. "It's only a bee. Nasty thing. It's dead now."

But Arjun sees that Rob hasn't made the connection between the ice cream and the bee. He believes he has been betrayed and he continues to wail.

Sunila has brought a piece of ice. Rob sucks, a strange rattling noisily incompatible with his weeping.

Arjun pitches his voice so that the boy will hear him. "Rob, son. The bee was on your ice cream. And when you put the ice cream into your mouth, you put the bee in, too. The bee was frightened and so it stung you."

Rob looks at his grandfather, his breath shaking his body, the piece of ice bulging from one cheek. "It bit me?"

"It stung you. Your mother pulled the sting out. The bee carries a sting in its tail."

"It stinged me?"

"Yes. You bit the bee and it stung you."

"I eated the bee." A smile wobbles across his face and Arjun wants to lift him into his arms. He nods instead, impatient with the knowledge that his arms won't even stretch out to his grandson.

Roxi gently wipes her son's face and cuddles him. "There, there, my darling."

Sunila sits close by. Arjun can see she also wants to do something to take away the pain.

It is at this moment that Arjun loves his wife, his daughter, with a flaming love that makes his chest hurt.

Sunila says, "I'll make some iced lemonade. That will make your tongue feel better, Robbie."

Arjun says, "Don't we have something? Give him medicine."

Sunila shakes her head and indicates Roxi with her chin. "They don't agree with that." *They* meaning Roxi's ex-husband, Hinton, who insists that pain doesn't exist; it's all psychological. Therefore, pain medication is irrelevant.

Arjun breathes in to steady himself and speaks quietly. "Roxi. Hinton isn't here. I don't think he'd mind since Rob is in so much pain."

She speaks into Rob's hair. "We don't give pain medicine. He threw them in the garbage. He said they killed people. He said he'd—" She looks up, startled. "Anyway, I think Robbie's feeling a bit better. Aren't you?"

Rob, still shaking with sobs, says, "Mm, mm."

Arjun wants to tell Sunila to go and get the damned medicine, but he can no longer make these commands. Not like Hinton, who is so much of a man that even in his absence the women will do what he says.

Arjun tries to remember. There was a time, wasn't there? There was a time when these women would have obeyed him. But his voice betrays the frailty of its owner. He is overruled by someone who isn't even part of their family anymore.

He makes himself breathe evenly, examining Rob's face for signs of swelling, for redness. There is some swelling around the eyes, but that may be because of the crying. He swallows past the hurtful obstruction in his throat. If he could open his mouth and take the pain, he would swallow it gladly.

Rob is quieter now. Sunila insists on peering into his mouth. Arjun is impatient with her. "You're poking around there as though you are after a rat."

"Be quiet. I'm trying to see if he's all right."

"Take him to the light where you can see better."

Sunila pushes her finger into Rob's mouth. He begins crying again. "I'm sorry, darling." She wipes her finger on her apron. "I think the swelling is going down."

"No thanks to you." Arjun wishes for the strength to cuff her. Foolish woman. And how foolish is Roxi sitting there, letting it happen?

The women croon over the crying child again. Arjun hates them and their *hush darling, no more crying darling*. Poor little Rob.

Finally, Roxi decides it's time to leave. Rob has fallen asleep. Arjun clears his throat for the request. "May I kiss him goodbye?"

There's a barely perceptible signal exchange between Roxi and Sunila. Arjun tries not to let the anger rise up. Roxi lowers the sleeping child so that Arjun can kiss the top of the sleeping child's head. He whispers, "Be well, son."

"What was that?" Sunila frowns at him.

Arjun shakes his head. This will be safe from her.

Sunila asks Roxi, "What did he say?"

Arjun says, "Have a safe journey, pet. Let us know when you get home."

He listens to the women talking their way out of the house. Their voices trail along the hedge outside as they walk out to the car. He hears Roxi open the car door and imagines her settling Rob in his car seat, buckling him in, nesting his cheek against the cushion. Goodnight, Rob.

He listens to the car starting up, the cheerful goodbyes, and the engine accelerating away. It is suddenly silent.

Sunila closes the front door and comes back into the living room. "Well, time for dinner I suppose. What do you want to eat?"

"Anything."

"All right," she says in her patient voice.

She goes to the kitchen, turns on her k.d.lang CD and clatters her pots and pans about. She will be absorbed there for another half hour.

He clutches his memories greedily. Rob's smile, his halo kiss, open-mouthed, sweet-breathed. His wonder at the elephants. His delight over everything. Arjun wonders, *Was I like that? Ever?*

He feels the painful stirring of anger against Hinton. What idiocy makes a man dismiss pain as though it is some fairytale? The arrogance of the young and fit. And how could these women go along with something so barbaric? The boy was in such pain.

Memory flings a door off its hinges. Roxi, thirteen, bent over and crying. They'd been getting ready for a trip to the beach. The car was packed, even Murad, notoriously slow at everything, was dressed and standing in the living room.

And now his daughter was crying. He saw his thirty-four year-old self, so confident, such authority, hands on hips. "Leave her, Sunila. She'll soon come around."

Sunila had murmured to Roxi, "I'll get you something."

He had shaken his head. "You're spoiling her."

Sunila had turned on him. "She's in *pain*."

"It's all in her mind."

He said that?

He hears the rattle of the tray approach, slow and then stop.

Sunila says, "Arjun?"

But he cannot reply; he weeps, bent over, as though he has dropped his heart somewhere in the folds of the blanket lying crumpled on the floor.

φ

Until Morale Improves
Rachel E. Pollock

I SWING THE CROP, LISTEN TO THE CRACK *as it connects. I smooth the shirt fabric gently back down across unflinching shoulders.*

This is not a real beating. It's just a scene.

Make no mistake: I am not titillated.

I swing the crop. I stroke the fabric.

I am not thinking of naughty children, nor bending some attractive young thing over my knee. If I feel anything, perhaps it's a touch of the blues.

Swing. Stroke.

I am not thinking of disciplined dogs, nor goading horses to gallop, nor even the brutalized boys of a prior century's Yorkshire schools, flogged to the brink of death by harsh headmasters like Wackford Squeers.

I deliver one more thrashing, my ears pricked up, but it still doesn't sound quite right.

I take a break, step back to reevaluate.

I should at least, I think, feel something for them, those whipped boys. I ought to think of them, decades-gone unfortunates beaten black and blue — but I can't. I'm just doing my job.

I work in the costume shop of a university theatre where we're currently producing the epic play, *The Life and Adventures of Nicholas Nickleby* — 748 pages of dense Dickensian prose translated into over six hours of theatre — and the actor who portrays poor, damaged Smike is to be beaten, for real, with an actual crop, before a live audience.

The scene is harrowing. Our Squeers is abhorrent, savage, our Smike wretched, so piteous it's been said that even the bored dilettantes from the criticism classes — notorious for rolling their eyes through first previews — were stunned into stillness, hands to mouths in shock.

He's not a genuine masochist, the actor, nor is he one of those Method types, so I've made him a protective backplate. The trouble is (as thousands of medieval knights could certes attest, if they yet lived to tell the tale), boiled leather sounds quite different from spongy flesh when struck. Upon it, the crop produces a hollow thock, a sturdy, resilient sound with none of the gutting resonance of scapular meat. The director fears it infringing upon the audience's suspension of disbelief, and it is my job to preserve the illusion.

I resume my castigation of the dressform's limbless torso with the soulless vigor of a mean drunk. I have no time for squeam or reticence; moderation wastes time, energy. I have to alter the backplate to elicit a bone-jarring smack by 4 p.m., when the final beating rehearsal is slated to take place. I've been doing this for nearly an hour. My arm's starting to hurt, and I'm fully aware that I could make five times my theatre salary swinging this crop against the shivering shoulder blades of pervy executives in an Alphabet City fetish club. I'm not thinking about that, though. Not much, at least.

I'm studiously ignoring the residents in the freshman dorm whose windows face my studio, bed-headed post-teens who awoke this morning pressing their hangovers into their temples and furling their shades to the sight of me, a bespectacled professor mercilessly flogging a trussed-up tailor's dummy. Later I'll discover that they've leapt in unison to their laptops, flooding the university's Facebook network with status updates of grainy cellphone pix captioned, "OMG HOLY WTF?!" (We couldn't pay for better viral marketing; tonight's performance will sell out.)

And what poetry, were I thinking about high art, but that would take liberty with fact. True, I thought about science and industry when I foraged through storage rooms for sections of blue foam and black rubber and clear plastic, cut them into back-shaped pieces, and began layering them in different configurations, all the while considering the physics of flagellation. And I thought about religion and faith when I remembered the seven hats I yet must finish trimming for tonight's photo call once this meaty-smack-pad is reconciled. High art, though, is but a speck on the cognitive horizon.

Psychology, too, takes its place in the cortege: in order to do this job, I've split myself in twain.

One half is a soldier stoically crouched in a front-line listening post. As crop strikes fabric strikes rubber strikes leather, this grim jarhead pays careful attention, focused only on the sonic particulars. Though the dress form feels nothing, I feel a vibration in the middle ear's trio of tiny bones, the hammer, anvil, and stirrup. *Malleus* strikes *incus* strikes *stapes* and the cochlean fluid quivers like poor, beaten Smike. The soldier analyzes: do I feel anything more?

Swing. Stroke.

No, I am not yet revolted, nor roused to compassion.

The beatings will continue.

While this professional listener takes meticulous notes, my other half musters a savagery I keep coiled tight, deep down. I prefer not to unfurl that part of human nature, but it happens onstage: so must it happen in my studio. Squeers holds nothing back when he beats our Smike — he deals it out with all the flesh-creeping relish of deSade — and perversely, now both a man's bodily safety and the illusion of his genuine harm lie in my two mild, pale hands.

Lips must quiver, tears must fall. Catharsis must steal up the aisles toward those who seek it.

So I cannot idly cane away in a desultory fashion, a sympathetic boatswain ordered to discipline a contrarian foremast jack. That will come later, when I wield my *malleus* — the cobbler's hammer I will use to rivet these layers together against my own actual anvil, my macro-*incus*. Later.

Now, some part of me has to lose myself, let fly an orgy of violence, lay into the narrow shoulders of this innocent dummy frothing with hate.

So I sack up and go for it. I attack with a ferocity that astounds my dissociated listening scout. Where did this brutality come from?

I'm thinking, as I swing the crop with all the viciousness I can muster, about my Aunt Mary.

Don't mistake: it's not that she was a horrible person, angry or vindictive or hateful — quite the opposite. She was peaceful, thoughtful, considerate, and kind. She was the first adult woman besides my own mother whom I considered a role model. She was witty, sarcastic, intelligent, rebellious, political, and spiritual. She was well-read, though she didn't much care for Dickens (too wordy and circuitous, a bit absurdist at times). We never saw eye-to-eye on that — I love his indulgently long sentences, his fantastical names and commedia characters with depth in the eyes behind their masks.

I use the past tense when speaking of Mary because she has recently died. Early in the production process of this show, in fact, she died swiftly of pancreatic cancer, grotesquely and in great pain, and it is clear I haven't yet begun to truly grieve, however much I might have cried already. Why else would she come to mind now?

I think about the fact that I'll never, ever see her again.

Swing. Stroke.

I think about how I felt when I heard she was dying, the terror that consumed me that I'd lose my uncle, too, to his own broken heart, or worse, by his own hand. (They'd never been apart, not since high school; this year would have been their 45th anniversary.)

Swing. Stroke.

I think about the day I got the call, that as soon as I hung up the phone, I had to put on a nice dress, go to an opening night gala, smile and schmooze and be witty over organic wines and intricate canapés.

Swing. Swing. Swing. Swing.

I wore a fun hat and cute shoes. I tossed my hair and smiled at the patrons, flirted with the benefactors and theatre critics. I got so drunk I threw up outside the stage door and fucked a guy I barely knew. When I run into him now, we pretend it never happened. For all I know, perhaps it didn't. After all, that's our collective *modus operandi* in the theatre: what's happening is only what you and I and everyone else in the room agrees to believe is happening.

These three people who barely know one another are actually a family, the Nickleby's, clad in black cloth, mourning the loss of a loved one. This man's a sadist; that man's a retard. This man beats that man within an inch of his life. We know it's not real, of course; we don't feel compelled to intervene, but yet we allow some portion of ourselves to believe in its truth—we invest enough verity in the experience that jaded pseudo-intellectuals buff away tears on the cuffs of their black turtlenecks as Smike cries out and cowers on the apron of the stage. So we could all agree to agree that I never puked on the loading dock, never banged that guy down the hall, and I'll buy that for the price of a ticket. Yes sirree. Too bad suspension of disbelief only works for the living. I could beg every person in the building to tell me Mary miraculously survived, but actual death yet trumps dramatic conceit.

I stand here with the crop in my hand, considering what I now believe to be the successfully-meaty backplate cover—three layers of neoprene skinned over with pigsuede—and think about grief, and loss, and the abject scrambling terror of my own mortality. I think about shame and I think about futility and I think about how powerless we all are in the face of such misery and fear.

And I begin to appreciate the therapeutic appeal of this contrived, harmless brutality.

Each time I rear back with the crop, another horror springs up: Mary, shouldering the Sisyphean burden of both the cancer and the drugs. Her husband, Bob, inchoate and inconsolable. My mother, losing her oldest friend. My father, unable to soothe his brother's pain. And myself, so far away and helpless, clinging to spectacle. I beat them back, these thoughts, let them go if only for a moment, and carefully smooth the shirt fabric gently back down in condolence.

I swing. I stroke.

φ

answer key: fact or fiction?

1. MY FATHER'S COURT : Fiction

"My Father's Court" is a piece of fiction that started in autobiography. When I was between eight and eleven, my father worked as janitor at the local high school, and he took me to some of the basketball games that he worked. He swept the floor with that wide broom (with the top of his undershorts sticking out above his belt), and he put a key in the wall to unlock the bleachers, which he drew forward or back like an accordion. I remember my mother as being generally unhappy (although my parents stayed married their whole adult lives), and there were probably real players who I looked at similarly to how the boy regards Tommy Bishop and Nate Williamson. Yet, "My Father's Court" is fiction. There were many nights with elements that found their way into this story, but there was never one night like this, with a game ending like this, or two players coming up afterwards to replay their moment of glory. There was never a moment where I had a ball in my hands and the choice to support my father or go against him. I do remember my father on his knees cleaning scuff marks off the wood floor with steel wool, but I have no idea how those scuff marks came to be. The father in this story is not my father; he's the boy's father as the boy-when-he's-no-longer-a-boy imagines him. I think this is one reason I prefer to write fiction: fiction can absorb fact into it, whereas I don't think fact can absorb fiction. Both, if they're any good, are true, and that's what I'd say about this story: it's fiction, and it's true. – Mark Farrington

2. CATCHING ATOMS : Fiction

Fiction, so often, is heavily infused with fact, though I'd argue the best stories free themselves of the "facts" at some point and, instead, adhere to the rules of the world of the story.

"Catching Atoms" was based on a schoolyard fight I witnessed as a child where one of the quietest, least significant boys in my class fought one of the most popular boys. Once I began writing the story, the characters—based on real people I had not seen or spoken to in years — began to round out into the characters they are now rather than versions of the people who inspired them. And as the characters grew more independent, the story became more real to me. Initially, I was exploring an event I remembered but did not truly understand. In having to get to know the entire world of the story, my growing understanding of it made it feel more authentic than my memory, allowing me to create details, such as Reece's 'Packy' jacket, that were true to the world of the story even if they never existed in the original event.

In the end, "Catching Atoms" is, to me, fictional because it is now very much its own story and not a retelling of the original event. – R. Dean Johnson

3. TATTLETALE : Non-Fiction

The writer of fiction knows how often "real" people, places and events crop up as one is imagining a story, and how the imaginations somehow twists and transforms these into a new creation. Conversely, the memoir writer, while trying to be faithful to reality, soon realizes that memory is a shifty thing, colored by time, emotions, repression and even often told family stories. In the end, what matters is the story itself — well crafted, vivid, somehow conveying a universal truth by means of a particular work of art. – Marian O'Shea Wernicke

4. OVER THE FALLS : Fiction

Sometimes they'll ask what it's like to write fiction and nonfiction. As if there's some great divide between the two. The dirty little secret? They are much closer aligned that we often care to acknowledge. Of course, narrative nonfiction must survive the fact-check of accuracy, while quality fiction usually is grounded in some character or world we can really believe in. But the best stories have many of the same elements – sense of place, memorable people, intriguing events. It's all a matter of how we choose to travel there. – Tim Wendel

5. Losing My Religion : Non-Fiction

There's very little that's clear cut in this life, especially when it comes to human beings and their thought patterns. Each time a memory is replayed in the mind, it's tweaked and adjusted and the new memory rewrites over the old. The ego also has a way of looking at The Truth through a self-serving lens. In that way, fiction can be more revealing than fact—like a dream, it reveals buried truths that the conscious mind can't or doesn't want to see. To me, a good story is a good story, whether fiction or nonfiction. It's up to you whether or not you trust the writer's intent—to present an experience in the world as he or she knows it. – Amy Fries

6. SACRAMENT : Non-Fiction

I've always said that going to the dentist is like going to confession. No matter how hard you protest that you've brushed and flossed, you can't disguise the truth – those black holes in your teeth tell all. But I guess nothing could be more confessional than getting naked with your priest. He sees all – but so do you. This story is a true confession; I was a young penitent seeking redemption when I entered into an affair with a Catholic priest. After a few years of secrecy and sin, he skulked away from the priesthood and we married. And after some dozen years of weirdness, psychological abuse and two scoops of crazy besides, I escaped, with children in tow. Today I confess that I have made many mistakes, but telling the truth isn't one of them. – Julia Park Tracey

7. BANTE : Fiction

I think one of the true pleasures of being a writer is the merging of fact and fiction. Perception is everything in our field. Put ten people in the middle of one single event and you'll get ten different stories. How can you not love that? But with ten versions, where is the truth? I do believe in the observable fact. If I stand in a rainstorm, I will get wet. But it's not the rainstorm that matters, it's ones reaction to it, whether it's transmuted into fiction or called memoir. – Ellen Bryson

8. MIRACLE : Fiction

When my son was about four years old, I'd be reading a story to him – something clearly fictional, such as Winnie-the-Pooh – and he'd turn to me and say, "I'm Winnie- the-Pooh." Even at that young age, he was able to recognize and articulate the power of fiction—the ability of fiction to incorporate the reader into the story. For this to happen, of course, the story has to ring true in some way. There has to be a truth beyond the implausible facts of talking stuffed animals living in the woods. My parents are immigrants from India. As I was growing up, they couldn't understand why I was turning out "American." We had many conflicts and arguments about the "American" things I wanted to do, such as date boys, live away from home at college, and hold part-time jobs during college. They could not understand my point of view, even though they had all the facts. It wasn't until I wrote an "autobiographical novel" for children, *Aruna's Journeys*, that they began to understand. This book has become one my mother's favorite books, even though the mother in the book is not particularly appealing. I think this is because my mother identified with the protagonist, the Indian-American girl, and became that girl as she read. Through this work of fiction, my mother was able to understand some of the truth of what I had experienced as a child. – Jyotsna Sreenivasan

9. BEATNIK : Non-Fiction

As a child, I lived inside of my imagination, turning myself into Superman one minute, a cowboy or heroic soldier the next. I didn't just imagine being someone else, I actually became that person, I was allowed to do this until third grade, that time in life when children are ordered to give up their imaginations and start living in the "real world." Teachers, parents, clergy, battered children, hoping to see their imaginations crumble and be reborn as "practicality."

Now, many years later, I urge students in fiction writing classes to reclaim their imaginations. They try hard to do that, only to discover that it's increasingly difficult, perhaps impossible, to sort fact from fiction, fiction from fact. Memoir, autobiography, journalism, blend into a Post Modern whirl; we quibble over genre. I say, let the critics decide what's what. I'm still a kid who loves telling stories, even if sometimes they happen to be true. – Fred A. Wilcox

10. FEELING FOR EGGS : Fiction

When I experience an event, I often think that I must write about it. I want to remember what I saw, what I felt. When writing fiction, I often find parts of my life blending in with imagined events and characters. In both kinds of writing, I invite the reader into my world. – Elizabeth Patton

11. FLYING WATERMELONS : Non-Fiction

"Flying Watermelons" was written shortly after I learned of the death of Billy in the story. When his wife subsequently asked me to write a eulogy for his memorial service, I asked if the piece could be humorous. She welcomed the idea, so I sent her "Watermelons," which I understand was read in its entirety at the service.

I filed the piece—along with dozens of other scribblings I had done over the years—in a folder labeled "Some Things That May Have Happened. "The genesis of every story in that file emerged from facts—at least as I remembered them. The passage of time probably contorted them in my mind, and the process of putting pen to paper may have altered them further, but I stand by the basics. Billy jumped that fence with two watermelons on his shoulders and buckshot in his butt. –Lawrence Russell

12. JOHN GREENWOOD : Fiction

My story "John Greenwood" is a work of fiction. Kind of. There was a phone call with my college friend that began "I had a dream about John Greenwood (not his real name)," but I can't remember which one of us said it. There was a date with the beautiful "John Greenwood," but he lost interest in me quickly, purportedly due to my sartorial faux pas (lime green Nikes).

The details of Valerie's life are entirely fabricated. Her core, however, represents an amalgam of people I've encountered in my life, damaged yet loving beings who can shoot a poison arrow that goes in so clean you don't feel it for days. The truth embedded in this piece of fiction is that regardless of who cocks the bow or catches the arrow, the point of origin is always fear. – Michelle Brafman

13. DETROIT : Non-Fiction

The designs auto manufacturers used in the 1950s and 1960s provided concrete images for the pent-up longings and fantasies of American youth. I grew up in Detroit, and I sought to recapture both the actual experience of perceiving those images and the reality of my own desire in this factual poem. – Edward Perlman

14. IF, THEN, BUT : Fiction

Pulp magazines of the '40s and '50s enticed readers with "True Confessions" in 48-point type on their covers (would their readers have turned away from "False Confessions"?). To rouse anti-Catholic sentiment, 'nuns' wrote confessional memoirs of their enslavement and abuse within 19th century convents. We never get a real confession from the protagonist of *The Confessions of Zeno*—he can't bare his soul to us because he can't confess anything to himself. We know this because Svevo (not the author's real name!) opens with Zeno telling us he's lighting his "last cigarette", even though he never quits.

So does true or false, fact or fiction, even matter? The Sonoran desert is part of the United States. It is also part of Mexico. But whichever side of the border you're on, it's still the desert. That's what I think about fact or fiction. Makes no difference. It's the story that counts, and the line has been blurry from day one. – George Nicholas

15. THE END OF THE SEASON : Fiction

In my writing the line between fiction and non-fiction is fixed and non-negotiable, even though the end purpose of both (one hopes) is truth. In non-fiction I *must* tell you when I'm lying whereas fiction is theatre—a risky, ambitious, elaborate and (sometimes) convincing fraud.

The line between 'fiction' and 'non-fiction' in our daily lives, however, is often murky—and I'm fascinated by human nature's ability to tolerate a disconnect between what we think and what we do, what we know and what we say. This small homage, (forgive me, Wharton and James), is an attempt to dramatize the consequential seasickness endured when one chooses to believe convenient lies and ignore inconvenient truths. In Gilded Age New York, an entire stratum of society depended on its members, like Mrs. Merrick, to have the good manners to do what was expedient, regardless of the consequences. Not so different from now, really." –Susan McCallum-Smith

16. AT THE DANCE : Fiction

I believe that all fiction is non-fiction. We are human and we draw on what we live and imagine. Truth, reality, longing, dream, these things are always blurred. We think we know what we've heard even if it is someone else's story, we feel we've lived what we've seen even if we weren't born then, and the one defining feature of all of it is the capacity within our minds to host what we believe to be true. Whether it happened or did not is immaterial. So did this happen? Yes it did. Exactly so? Yes. This is exactly as it was. – Ru Freeman

17. CARELESS FISH : Fiction

I happen to believe that fiction is truer than nonfiction, that heart beats out fact—always, no matter the weather. So is my story true? Well, yeah. It's true. In a parallel universe to ours, one in which there is meaning to every action, consequence and resonance in each inaction. That's not our world, the real world. Sure, my family and friends would notice if I fell from a suspension bridge into a river. But would that moment matter to our world or hold revelation? Of course not. Well, momentary revelation; I may—note, *may*—have stopped seeing the boy whose jostling dumped me off the bridge. Personal resonance is a rare thing in life. But good short stories hold this gift all the time and I eat it up because it's the closest thing my collection of atoms will ever come to life in a state of order and grace. That's why I read, that's why I write. "Careless Fish" holds a number of details born of my own reality: my family lived at a lake where a boy had become paralyzed when he hit a submerged trash can while swimming. He was suing the lake board and my father did, for a time, sit on that board. I used to sneak in my brother's room to stare at his magazines and once or twice stole one away for a while. And there was a boy like the boy in "Careless Fish." Still, I am not the protagonist and her story is not mine. Her story is the truth. – Nicole Louise Reid

18. THE LAST TIME : Non-Fiction

So often have I read something and wondered, is this true, and the opposite as well. Is this really fiction? I'm intrigued by this. Why does it matter to me? Am I a voyeur? Am I inherently distrustful? I wrote a novel based on my prison experience in Colombia. Over the course of working on it for a period of five years, I began to realize that certain events had grown murky. I could no longer remember whether they had actually happened as described in the story. If I were to write a memoir, I knew that relying on my memory would at best be faulty. "The Last Time," which I do recall clearly, I think, came to me in the middle of the night. I wrote it in a few hours, images rising into my mind as though they had all happened yesterday. And, for all intents and purposes, they did. – Herta B. Feely

19. DESIRE : Non-Fiction

My essay, "Desire," is about what we deny to ourselves. I think the only way to find out what we're repressing is to start writing. I reveal my mother as someone who doesn't like herself, her husband, or me and as someone who denies and represses her true feelings in convoluted ways. Or at least that's what I think she was doing. And I think I learned to do the same thing—and then one day, I began to write about my divorce and found out what I believe to be fact. Confessions. Would my mother agree? Who knows? She's ashes in the wind. – Elly Williams

20. THE GRASS WIDOW : Non-Fiction

As a journalist for more than three decades, I once wrote in a column that "Memory is a tricky thing. Truth is not." The 2006 piece focused on Oprah Winfrey's selection of James Frey's book, *A Million Little Pieces*, which, as it turned out, contained more fiction than fact. The Doubleday "memoir" spawned a troubling new term dubbed "faction," a deliberate mesh of truth and lies. The ensuing debates created other curious concepts of "emotional truth," "truthiness," and "altered details." The controversy begged the question "when is a lie not a lie?"

With memoir, as some of my classmates at Johns Hopkins University argued, a writer cannot honestly trust their memory; it is not possible to recall what happened years ago. The key is to be transparent about your fuzziness with warning phrases such as "as near as I can recall," or "in my child's mind," or "as memory serves me now." Otherwise, you're writing fiction. The impetus for fiction often begins with fact. However, when you embellish or distort the facts to protect the innocent or the guilty, and the real people take on fictional lives of their own, then call them "characters," and label that invention for what it truly is, a confession. – A. Terrell Washington

21. THEY SHALL BE COMFORTED : Fiction

Perhaps it is more how we write about fact or fiction. Some people can recall specific chronology by certain things that surround an event. Some are affected by the senses or by related memories. In other words, how can one person's version of an eclipse be the same as another's?

Even if we agree on the date of an event, such as an earthquake, there will be someone who might have had a premonition or a dream that foreshadowed the event. If so, then for that person the earthquake didn't begin at the time of the measured temblor but at some point prior to that. How we receive information is deeply significant and, for me, more fascinating. – Sandra Hunter

22. UNTIL MORALE IMPROVES : NON-FICTION

Exposures of "literary fraud" when it comes to falsified memoirs fascinate me in their potential for tragedy, in my imagination at least. What is so dissatisfactory about these authors' actual lives, that they actively create alter egos in such a risky public forum? And how horribly compounded that dissatisfaction must be when the control of those alter-egos spiral out into the realms of recognition that writers like James Frey and "JT Leroy" experienced? I have to wonder, mightn't they all have been saved tarring with the impostor-brush by a simple change of genre? I have no answers to these questions. I do know this: it is both exhilarating and terrifying to lead a life in which truth is so often, far and away, stranger than fiction. Every time I find myself in a situation like the one I've written for this anthology, I ask myself: is this reality, or am I secretly deluded? – Rachel E. Pollock

author biographies

Michelle Brafman's fiction has received numerous honors, including a Special Mention in the 2010 *Pushcart Prize Anthology*, South Million Writer's Award listing as one of the best online stories published in 2009, and nominations for a 2011 Pushcart Prize and *Best New American Voices 2009*. A past winner of the F. Scott Fitzgerald Short Story Contest, her stories have appeared in *The Minnesota Review, Lilith Magazine, Gargoyle, Blackbird Literary Journal, Fifth Wednesday Journal*, and other publications. She teaches creative writing at George Washington University and lives in Glen Echo, Maryland with her husband and two children.

Ellen Bryson holds a BA in English from Columbia University and an MA in creative writing from Johns Hopkins University in Washington, DC. She is the author of *The Transformation of Bartholomew Fortuno*, a novel about being different, being human, and finding redemption. After a career as a professional modern dancer, she shifted her focus to the philanthropic field where she worked for over a decade in both private and community foundations, culminating in national work for the Council on Foundations in Washington DC. A world traveler, she has lived in the Middle Eastern country of Bahrain and in Argentina. Although she and her husband currently live in San Diego, they are considering a move to France.

Mark Farrington has taught fiction writing in the Johns Hopkins M.A. in Writing Program for the past fifteen years. He has an M.F.A. from George Mason University, where he studied with Richard Bausch and such visiting writers as Jane Smiley and Tim O'Brien. His short fiction has won a Virginia Commission on the Arts Individual Artists Fellowship, the Dan Rudy Fiction Prize, the Metroversity Fiction Award, and second place in the Dame Alice Throckmorton Prize, and has been published in *The Louisville Review, The New Virginia Review*, and other journals. He has also published numerous articles on writing and the teaching of writing, and is a Teacher Consultant with the Northern Virginia Writing Project, an affiliate of the National Writing Project. "My Father's Court" was previously published at coffeehousefiction.com.

Herta B. Feely is an award winning writer and editor. In 2010, she received the American Independent Writers award for best published personal essay, and for her novel *Serra Blue* she was awarded both the James Jones First Novel Fellowship and an Artist Fellowship in Literature from the D.C. Commission on the Arts & Humanities. Her short fiction and memoir pieces have been published in assorted literary journals, including *The Sun, Lullwater Review, Provincetown Magazine, The Potomac Review,* and *Big Muddy.* In 2002, she received a Master of Arts in Writing from Johns Hopkins University. "The Last Time" is from her memoir in progress *Far From Home.* Information regarding her editorial services is on her website and blog: www.chrysaliseditorial.com.

Ru S. Freeman was born in Colombo, Sri Lanka. She attended college and graduate school in Australia, the United States and Sri Lanka. Her political writing appears in English and Arabic. Her creative work has appeared or is forthcoming in *Guernica, Story Quarterly, Crab Orchard Review, World Literature Today, Pebble Lake Review* and elsewhere and was nominated for the Best New American Voices anthologies in 2006 and 2008. She was selected to represent the US, along with four other writers, in China during the summer of 2010, through the Iowa University International Writing Program. She is a contributing editorial board member of the *Asian American Literary Review.* Her debut novel *A Disobedient Girl* has been long-listed for the DSC South Asian Literary Prize.

Amy Fries is a writer and editor working in Northern Virginia. She is a blogger for PsychologyToday.com and the author of *Daydreams at Work* (Capital Books, 2009). Amy received a Master of Arts in Writing from Johns Hopkins University.

Sandra Hunter's short fiction has appeared in the *New Delta Review, Zyzzyva, Talking River Review, the South Dakota Review, Glimmer Train* (awards in 2005, 2006, 2007, 2008, 2010), and others, and has been nominated for a Pushcart Prize. Her novel *Leaving to Come Home* placed as a semi-finalist in the 2010 Dana Novel of the Year Award and as a finalist in the 2010 Southwest Writers Contest, Literary Novel Category. "They Shall Be Comforted" is a chapter from her novel-in-progress titled *Waiting for Heaven*.

R. Dean Johnson lives in Kentucky with his wife, the writer Julie Hensley, and their son. He is an assistant professor in the Brief-Residency MFA Program at Eastern Kentucky University. His essays and stories have appeared in, among others, *Juked, Natural Bridge, New Orleans Review, Slice,* and *The Southern Review.* "Catching Atoms" originally appeared, in a slightly different version, in *Ruminate.*

Susan McCallum-Smith is an award-winning writer of fiction, non-fiction, and reviews. Her work has been featured in *Urbanite, The Philadelphia Inquirer, The Scottish Review of Books,* and *The Gettysburg Review,* and anthologized in *City Sages* and *The Pushcart Prize Anthology.* Her reviews are often heard on Maryland Public Radio and she hosts the "Belles Lettres Review Blog." She received her degrees in creative writing from Johns Hopkins and Bennington College. *Slipping the Moorings,* her short story collection, was published in early 2009 by Entasis Press. She was born in Scotland and currently lives in the United States.

George Nicholas, a graduate of U.C. Irvine's MFA program and a former advertising creative director, writes speeches, radio and TV spots, short films and fiction from his office in Washington, D.C. His business website is workinguy.com. Guilty pleasures can be found at web.me.com/gnofdc1.

Elizabeth Patton was born and educated in the South, and taught English in New York. Her work has appeared in *The New York Times, Christian Science Monitor, Yankee Magazine* and a wide variety of literary magazines, anthologies and professional journals. In fall 2009, her poetry chapbook, *Late Harvest,* was published by Pudding House Press.

Edward Perlman, a resident of Washington DC, is the poetry advisor and program coordinator for the Master of Arts in Writing degree at Johns Hopkins University; he is also the owner and publisher of Entasis Press, a literary press publishing fiction, nonfiction, and poetry.

Rachel E. Pollock is a professor of Costume for Dramatic Art at the University of North Carolina, Chapel Hill. Her creative writing has appeared in the *Harvard Summer Review, Southern Arts Journal*, and *Main Channel Voices*, as well as the anthologies *Voices of Multiple Sclerosis, Imagining Heaven*, and *Knoxville Bound*. She is also the sole author of the professional weblog, "La Bricoleuse: Costume Craft Artisanship" (http://labricoleuse.livejournal.com/).

Nicole Louise Reid is the author of the novel *In the Breeze of Passing Things* (MacAdam/Cage) and fiction chapbook *Girls* (RockSaw Press). Her stories have appeared in *The Southern Review, Quarterly West, Meridian, Black Warrior Review, Confrontation, turnrow*, and *Crab Orchard Review*. Recipient of the Willamette Award in Fiction, she teaches creative writing at the University of Southern Indiana, where she is editor of RopeWalk Press, fiction editor of Southern Indiana Review, and directs the RopeWalk Visiting Writers Reading Series. "Careless Fish" first appeared in *Crab Orchard Review* (vol. 8, no. 1; fall/winter 2002).

Lawrence Russell was born in Brooksville, Florida, was educated at the University of Florida, and spent 35 years living and working in eight countries as an American Foreign Service Officer. He published a piece based on that experience in the *Foreign Service Journal*, entitled "How I Came to Love Cockroaches." He is spending his retirement years in Washington, D.C.

Jyotsna Screenivasan's short fiction has appeared or is forthcoming in *American Literary Review, Bellowing Ark, Catamaran, Concisely, Green Hills Literary Lantern, India Currents, Iron Horse Literary Review, Nassau Review, Phantasmagoria, Tampa Review*, and *Tiferet*. One story has been anthologized in *Living in America: South Asian American Writers*.

Another story will be included in a parenting anthology published by City Works Press of San Diego. She the author of two novels for children, as well as two reference books, *Utopias in American History* and *Poverty and the Government in America*, both published by ABC-CLIO. She has received grants from the Washington, DC Commission on the Arts and Humanities. Jyotsna currently lives in Moscow, Idaho with her husband and sons, and works at the University of Idaho.

Julia Park Tracey is an award-winning writer, editor and journalist. Her novel, *Tongues of Angels*, appeared in 2002 from Scarlet Letter Press. Her award-winning column, "Modern Muse," appears monthly in the *Alameda Sun* newspaper, which she co-founded in 2001; the "Modern Muse" blog is online (www.modernmuse.blogspot.com); in 2007, she received the East Bay Press Club's award for best independent blogger. Her essays, articles and reviews have appeared in numerous publications, including *The Sun* and the *San Francisco Chronicle*. Her poetry has appeared in numerous literary journals and books of poetry, including the *PEN West Anthology* (2007), *Americas Review, Atticus Review, Cicada, Green Fuse, Sacred River, Prophetic Voices, Protea Poetry Journal, New Cicada* (Japan), *Tattoo Highway* and others.

A. Terrell Washington, a native Washingtonian, is an award-winning journalist, professor, speaker and historian. She is a columnist and editorial writer for the Afro-American Newspapers (Afro.com), a former columnist and editor for *The Washington Times* and a political commentator for WRC-TV/NBC. She is an adjunct professor at The Catholic University of America and at the University of the District of Columbia's community college. A graduate of Johns Hopkins University with a master's degree in writing, she is the owner of Awash-n-Words, a freelance writing business and is an affiliate of the Amherst Writers and Artist. She is co-founder of the Ft. Ward and Seminary African American Descendants Group, and is currently pursuing a doctoral degree in education for adult learners.

Tim Wendel is the author of eight books, including the novels *Castro's Curveball* and *Red Rain*. His most recent title *High Heat: The Secret History of the Fastball and the Improbable Search for the Fastest Pitcher of All Time* was critically acclaimed by *The New York Times Book Review*,

The Boston Globe and *Sports Illustrated*. His writing has appeared in *Esquire, GQ, Washingtonian, The New York Times* and *The Washington Post*, as well as the literary journals *The Potomac Review* and *Gargoyle*. A graduate of Johns Hopkins University, he teaches nonfiction and fiction writing there. This story was an excerpt from his novel, *Over the Falls*.

Marian O'Shea Wernicke has been the faculty editor of *The Hurricane Review*, a national literary magazine published by Pensacola Sate College, for the past seven years. She is a recently retired professor of English at the college, and participated at the Sewanee Writers Conference in workshop with Maxine Kumin and Mark Jarman. She writes poetry and fiction and is now working on a memoir about her father.

Fred A. Wilcox is an honors graduate of the Iowa Writers Workshop, teaches full time in the Writing Department at Ithaca College, and is the author of several works of nonfiction, including *Chasing Shadows: Memoirs of a 'Sixties Survivor*, and *Waiting for an Army to Die: The Tragedy of Agent Orange*. Seven Stories Press will bring out *Scorched Earth: Legacies of Chemical Warfare* in spring or fall 2011.

Elly Williams is the author of the novel *This Never Happened*, also published in the UK under the title *Crazy Think*. Her short story, "The Yellow Bathrobe," was anthologized in *Of Grace and Gravity*. The *Mississippi Review* and *Five Points* have both published interviews by Dr. Williams. She received her MA in Writing from Johns Hopkins and her PhD in English from the University of Ohio. She teaches in the Advanced Academic Programs in Writing for Johns Hopkins and for the English Department at Hood College. She has taught at and been a Fellow at Sewanee and the Hambidge Center among other places, and she received the Jackobson Scholarship from Wesleyan University in recognition of her current work-in-progress. She also is the Director and Founder of the Hood College Young Writers' Conference. "Desire" is from her memoir *Collision*.

acknowledgements

Putting together this anthology was a challenging (while fun!) undertaking. Thank you, especially, to the following people:

Amanda Vacharat for her incredible energy and persistence, her creativity (she designed the cover), and her unrelenting sense of perfection.

George Nicholas for the cover photo (courtesy of the estate of Aristedes Nicolau) and for direction on the cover's design.

Sheri Jiang for helping to read the stories, organize the files, and put us on the road to a finished product.

All the authors for their patience, artistry, and insights into fact and fiction.

To all of you we are most grateful.

Breinigsville, PA USA
27 December 2010
252246BV00001B/3/P

9 781609 106096